JOSEPH *was a*

Loving Father

JOSEPH *was a*
Loving Father

VINCENT IEZZI

LEONINE PUBLISHERS
PHOENIX, ARIZONA, USA

Published by Leonine Publishers LLC
Phoenix, Arizona
USA

ISBN-13: 978-1-942190-23-3

Library of Congress Control Number: 2015959901

Printed in the United States of America
10 9 8 7 6 5 4 3 2 1

Cover design by Tom Pelle, Tamarin Entertainment
www.tamarinent.com

Visit us online at www.leoninepublishers.com
For more information: info@leoninepublishers.com

to my son,
Robert Joseph Iezzi,
who has been a loving father

Introduction

This work is one of fiction based on fact.

Every author tries to make his book informative and as close to the facts as possible. I am no exception, but sometimes things in the present do not equal things from the past. Words and titles are written that do not convey the same idea as is intended. One case is the word *Rabbi*. I wrote the title with my deepest respect, for I have several close friends who are Rabbis, but the way we understand Rabbi today is not the way it was understood at the time of Joseph. In the past it was not associated with synagogue ministry, as with the Catholic priesthood or like a Protestant minister, but one of teacher, "a ruler of the synagogue." So, as my dear readers progress through my story, I hope they understand that my use of the word, Rabbi, is meant as a title of respect for the individual and not the full present day definition. It is to convey the idea of a man of holiness and wisdom and a leader.

Now we come to another point of interpretation. The Hebrew ceremony of the *Bar Mitzvah* as we know it today was not in place at the time of Jesus or Joseph. There was a ceremony which was called "The Blessing and Praise" which took the young man into full relationship with God, but was not celebrated as it is today among our Hebrew brethren. So as you progress through my story, you will find the absence of a *Bar*

Mitzvah and the entry of "Blessing and Praise" for this reason. Rest comfortable in the idea that both ceremonies were to convey that beautiful time when a young Hebrew boy becomes a Hebrew man and in communion with his God.

In this book I use many Hebrew terms and that is to give more flavor and reality to my story. This is an author's privilege and I revel it in and enjoy it freely. I have followed the Hebrew or Latin terms with translations so as to help you enjoy the book more. When Hebrew words are used by a Hebrew speaker, I do not use italic for it is not a foreign word to them; but when I used any Hebrew words in description or commentary, I italicize the word and follow with the English translation.

The storyline of this book is the result of many, many hours of private meditation in Holy Hours and in Scripture reading. The conclusions of the book are my own conclusions, or private revelations. When researching for confirmation of my conclusions, I found much of my thinking in a number of Apocryphal writings. I have had a great Catholic education, from grade school through college, and I do not believe I have created any heresy or dogmatic errors. I submit everything to the Church's Magisterium. If you disagree with my conclusions I beg your forgiveness and ask for your prayers. If you agree, then I praise God for offering me confirmation.

This book took a long time to write because of the research. It has been a blessing as all my books have been because I found more truths than doubts in my research and for that I am eternally pleased. The diligence and patience and professionalism of my editor and publisher are commendable and appreciated beyond words. I give them my humble and eternal thanks.

Finally, I wrote this book because I always felt Saint Joseph was the least appreciated, remembered, and recognized saint in my Church, despite his heroic actions. It seems so unfair, so I set out to help make things right. He was a plain man like so many of us with no great qualities other than what he had been given. His faith was as strong as any other saint in our long history. I was overjoyed to see him recently placed in the Canon of Mass and rejoice at each Mass when I hear his name read out. He was an example far greater than recognized because he was just a father and many times fathers are willingly overlooked. I hope you hear Joseph's voice as you read this book.

To me Saint Joseph is the patron saint of faith and I encourage all who have problems, doubts, egos, or any spiritual malady to *Ite ad Ioseph*—go to Joseph.

Finally, there is the use of the word, "God." Our Hebrew family has the greatest respect for the Name of God, something many Christians fail to do and have not been humble, respectful enough to adopt. A Hebrew would never speak or write the name of God. So they used other titles to give the idea of God but not the sound of His Name. You will find *Adonai, El Shaddai* through the book. These words mean Lord, The Almighty. I pray this is not cumbersome for you— that you accept it in the same respect that our Hebrew brethren intend.

Pace e bene. Peace and good.

T

Joseph Was a Loving Father

The cry of a baby pierced the peaceful spring morning.

Jacob smiled with pride. Straightening his back and squaring his shoulders, he took a deep breath. His short muscular body showed no signs of aging, except his graying hair and beard. He and his wife had begun having children late in their marriage.

From the strong sound of the crying baby, he knew he had another son. He stood looking at the heavy woolen brown curtain that separated him from his child and Eva, his wife. He waited patiently, yet delightedly, for one of the town's *meyaledot*—midwives—to appear to confirm the birth of his new son. Again, he heard the zealous cry of the baby and Jacob grew more excited and more certain that his new son was sturdy, with a strong mind and a need to be heard.

Several moments later, the curtain that separated the two rooms was drawn back, and Arella the Elder, the midwife, walked into the room carrying the child.

"Yakov, your wife Chava has presented you another son," Arella said, smiling and pleased to share such good news with him.

Jacob extended his arms, for they ached and yearned to hold the new life in his family.

Arella carefully placed the naked baby in his arms.

He looked down at the baby, whose alert brown eyes stared back at him in apparent recognition. The baby's steady stare was broken only when his eyes toured the room, examining for the first time the world around him. Finally, his attention returned to Jacob's face. With a quick, small pleased smile and a sigh of contentment, he accepted Jacob as his father. The baby still had the signs of a newborn, and Jacob relished the aroma of new life as it entered his lungs and slowly seeped through his body and senses. He carefully placed the child "upon his knees." This custom showed recognition of the legitimacy of a child. In a low, yet audible whisper, Jacob spoke from Holy Scriptures the words: "Unto us a child is given…" The smallness of his voice showed his gratitude and his eyes filled with tears of joy.

Arella walked to him and gently took the child from him. "He has to be washed, rubbed with salts to thicken his skin, and then wrapped in swaddling clothes," she said with professional authority. "After Chava breastfeeds him, you shall see him again, and you will be able to visit with Chava, and thank her for bearing this gift, another son, for you."

Jacob watched as she took his child from the room, through the curtain again. He stood basking in the aura of new fatherhood, in growing appreciation of his wife and of this new gift.

Suddenly he turned, rushed to the door of the house, and called his older son Cleopas to him. Cleopas, who had been patiently waiting nearby, came running to his father. When he saw the smile on his father's face, he knew he had a brother. Excitedly Jacob instructed the boy to go to the homes of their relatives and their friends in the village to tell them of the birth of his new son. After all the family and friends had been told the news, Cleopas was instructed to go to the house of Chaniel, the *mohel*,—person who circumcises—and tell the old man that in eight days a circumcision was to be done. With a big smile on his face, the boy obeyed. He sprinted from the house, filled with the importance of his news and his duty.

Jacob turned and reentered the house. He walked directly to a small stool in the corner of the room. He sat and leaned his back against the wall. He began to think:

Now, Adonai—Lord, I come to You and give You the praise and thanksgiving that is due only to You. Forgive me if I hurried to do other things before I thanked You, but my human mind was working as a father, and not as Your son.

He closed his eyes and claimed all the stillness he could. Having found a place where he knew he could find God, he slowly, reverently covered his head with his hood, closed his eyes and raised his hand to the heavens. Aloud he chanted a Psalm:

"Baruch Atah Adonai. Erachamcha na Adonai.

Blessed art Thou, O God! I love Thee, O Lord,

my strength . . . O Lord, my rock; my fortress, my

deliverer. My God, my rock of refuge, my shield, the

strength of my salvation, my stronghold! I will call

upon the Lord, most praiseworthy, and I will be safe

from my foes . . ."

His moment was interrupted by Arella as she pushed the heavy drape from the door way. Her presence in his space distracted him and he knew his time with God was lost. When she realized he had finished his prayers, the old woman said, "So Yakov, what shall this son of yours be called?"

Jacob looked at her for several pensive moments then sitting upright, he squared his shoulders and announced loudly: "He shall be called Yosef, which means 'He will increase.'"

Arella smiled and nodded her head repeatedly. "So it is. He shall be Yosef."

Joseph's thirteenth birthday was the first memorable birthday of his life. It was the year of his *Barchot ve Tefillot*—Blessing and Prayers—the year he became a "son of the commandment" and a man. From the age of five he had been preparing for this all-important day. Jacob had done his fatherly duty by retelling, and on occasions, reading Joseph stories from the *Torah*, the Five Books of Moses. When Jacob prayed, reciting from memory the Psalms or verses and blessings from the *Torah*, he always demanded that his sons Cleopas and Joseph stand with him and listen and repeat what was said. Every male relative or neighbor who came to the house and partook of meals or participated in prayers would recite their Psalms aloud too, so the boys would hear and memorize them. In this way, Joseph came to know all that he had heard. Above all else, during this time, Jacob taught his son the importance of being Hebrew and of being part of the Chosen People.

When he had reached his tenth year, Joseph had begun to attend classes at the *Beth ha-Sefer*—the village's synagogue school. Here, under the watchful eyes of Rabbi Delayoh, he learned *Eevreet*—Hebrew—and the *Tanakh*—Bible. Jacob had then taken a secondary role, and had spoken to Joseph of the *minhag*—the traditions of their people. At the school, under the strict teachings of Rabbi Delayoh, young Joseph had felt a personal closeness with *El Shaddai*—The Almighty. While other children, and even adults, spoke of God with an edge of fearful respect in their voice, Joseph felt at ease with Him.

When he prayed or spoke of God, he believed he should be himself. He had the same respect that the others had; everyone could see it, but Joseph was thought to have strong insights of God. Many times when he spoke of Him, people would stand in wonder of his thoughts. Joseph felt that God was pleased with him, and approved of his familiarity. Praying: talking to God, seemed natural and normal, like speaking to an old trusted friend or elderly relative. Often Joseph would sit down and speak to a vacant stole, for he was sure God was there as He was everywhere.

When he spoke of God in the presence of others, he followed all the prescribed acts of respect, such as bowing and covering his head, yet when alone, he would apologize to God for not being relaxed in His public prayers. He never told anyone about the way he felt for he knew that this would bring severe reprimands upon him. Joseph felt this connection was for him alone, and it was to remain his secret.

On the day of his Blessings and Prayers, Joseph walked with his father, uncles, brother, and other male relatives and neighbors to the synagogue. He wore his brother Cleopas's sandals and white and blue trimmed robe but the *tallit*—prayer shawl, which his mother had made for this occasion, was his and his forever-more.

The *Beyt Knesset*—Synagogue assembly—was a rectangular hall with columns that divided the room into three sections. The larger and wider center section was bracketed by the two smaller sections. The décor was very simple: the walls were stucco and white, deco-rated with paintings of green Nile palm trees, soft pink feathers, and five or six pointed stars scattered here and there. A replica of the *menorah*—seven-branched candelabra—and several small light blue stars were painted on the ceiling of the room between the thick dark wood rafters.

Rows of wooden benches, most without backs, lined each side of the center section. These seats, facing each other, were for the men of the congregation. Two or three rows of benches in the back of the room behind a wooden screen faced the altar. Behind this screen sat the female members of the synagogue.

In the center of the room on the bare earth, a rug partially covered the ground before the main platform. It was the most expensive thing in the building and had been purchased many years ago from a caravan of Persians who had passed by the village. The rug was dark blue, and white scrolls decorated the edges. It was meticulously kept clean and few people were permit-ted to step on it. Those to wed, those presenting babies for blessings, and males set for the Blessing and Prayers were the rare ones allowed to stand on the rug.

Joseph was left standing alone on the large expensively woven rug. He was aware that everyone's thoughts and eyes were on him. He heard the low mumbles of the men, and sensed his father's pride and his brother's camaraderie. From behind the large screen that separated the men from the women, he could feel his mother's warmth on his cheek.

Unexpectedly, Joseph felt all the ancients of Israel there with him. He felt surrounded and embraced by the famous and not so famous that had been blessed to follow God. He was certain that every male Hebrew had felt this on the day of their Blessing and Prayers, yet this moment was his and that made it different. Abruptly from somewhere beyond him, he experienced a breath passing over him; he grasped it and held it, willingly accepting it as a supernatural happening. The breath warmed him and Joseph felt the caress of the love of God. It settled upon him and saturated him. He understood this to be something singular; and from that day on, he knew that he had something exclusive to do for God. He did not need to know what he was to do, in fact, he was sure this knowledge would come much later in life, yet at that moment, he became aware of a mission before him.

He confidently raised his eyes and looked at the *bimah*—platform—and beyond to the *Aron Kodesh*—the cabinet holding the Torah. He uttered a small prayer, asking God that he be ready to do what was asked of him. He closed his eyes and felt the presence of a Greatness so enormous that every fiber of his being tingled with excitement. Moments passed. Peace came over him, and he acknowledged that he would be forevermore in God's presence.

His thoughts were interrupted by the sound of Rabbi Delayoh's booming voice calling him by his full Hebrew name. He solemnly lifted his prayer shawl from his shoulders and placed it over his head, then let the white woolen cloth drape and frame his glowing face. He walked slowly to the *bimah* and grasped the wooden rollers of the *Torah*, one in each hand. He looked out at those present, and in a clear and melodious voice chanted:

> "Barechu et Adonai Hamevorach.
> Baruch Adonai Hamevorach L'olam Va-ed.
>
> Praise the Lord, to whom all praise is due!
>
> Praise the Lord, to whom our praise is due
>
> now and forever!"

He was a Hebrew man.

From that day on, he grew his beard and left the hair on his head to grow. At home that night, when all the well-wishers had departed, Joseph recited the *Shema*—Hebrew declaration of faith—with Jacob and Cleopas. Until the day he died, he faithfully recited it twice a day. He covered his eyes with his right hand as the memorized prayer came from his mouth. He spoke with great strength and the breath of new life. His voice was filled with emotions. His inner being with its entire intellect came to life. His chest swelled with pride, his eyes moistened with tears, and his voice rang clearly for he heard, knew and believed the words of this prayer for the first time.

"Sh'ma Yis' ra'eil Adonai Eloheinu Adonai echad.
Arukh sheim k'vod malkhuto l'olam va'ed.

Hear, Israel, the Lord is our God, the Lord is One.

Blessed be the Name of His glorious kingdom for

ever and ever."

Soon his father's and brother's voices blended with his as Joseph welcomed the beginning of his manly journey in life.

Joseph felt the perspiration on his head, and was aware of the beads of sweat rolling down his face into his shallow black beard. It was an oppressively warm day in Nazareth, but it was a day that demanded more of him than usual. He had to complete this yoke for Nachum, the farmer, who was in dire need of it for his oxen. The urgency of the job kept Joseph deep in thought and work. He reached for his hone and began to sharpen his chisel. Then he reached for his mallet and carefully knocked the chisel into the wood, smoothing a rough spot. He slowly moved his hand over the area, and was satisfied that he had corrected the problem.

"Yosef, is Yakov home?" The booming voice of Rabbi Delayoh jolted Joseph from his task, but he quickly regrouped his thoughts and without looking up answered, "Shalom, Rabbi. Yes, he is with my Immi— mother."

"How have you been, Yosef? I hear your brother, Chaleph—Cleopas, is a father again. It is a berakah— blessing—for Yakov."

"Yes, and we are all happy for Chaleph and his wife, Maryam," Joseph replied, as he continued with his work. He deeply respected the Rabbi, but the yoke was heavy on his mind, and he knew that the man of God was only being polite by making small talk for he only had meaningful conversations with fathers and elders. Without looking up from his work, Joseph knew just how he looked.

The Rabbi was a short, chunky man. His face was round, surrounded by long hair and *peyos*—long side-burns. His beard was as white as the snow. The only flesh one saw of his face was a small, pointed nose and dark brown eyes that peered out from beneath heavy eyebrows. His short arms and small fat fingers were folded and resting on his extended stomach at all times, even when he walked. The front of his robe was raised by his ample stomach, revealing his bony white ankles and sandaled feet. He walked slowly and timidly as if in great pain, which he was not, but he liked to make people believe he was suffering.

Finished with his niceties, the Rabbi ambled to the doorpost, touched the *mezuzah* on the right portal of the doorway, and announced himself as he entered the house.

Joseph, certain that the Rabbi would be quickly received by his parents in their usual respectful way, continued with his chore and forgot the interruption.

Inside the house, after the usual small talk, Rabbi Delayoh announced solemnly, "Yakov, it is time."

"Rabbi, you speak in riddles. What is it time for, may I ask?" Jacob spoke with a diplomatic smile to hide his irritation.

"It is time for Yosef to think of marriage."

A weighty silence filled the room.

"He is of age and I have an almah—maiden—whose parents are willing to make a marriage contract with you."

Jacob was distracted by the entrance of his wife Eva, who had pushed the heavy curtain of the doorway aside and stood silently and respectfully by the doorpost. Jacob knew she had been listening to the conversation; she always did. He knew from the look on her face that she was bothered by the Rabbi's announcement. It seemed just days ago that they had married off their first son, Cleopas, and now their *tinok*—baby—was to follow.

"He is seventeen," Jacob said. His remark was more like an objection than an announcement. He quickly cleared his throat and continued, "And the maiden, how old is she? Who are her parents?"

"She is fourteen and the daughter of Benyamin bar Gibor, the katzav—butcher. Her name is Melcha. She is a good choice. She is beautiful, respectful, a good Jewess and a good housekeeper."

"I thank you for this information," Jacob quickly said as he looked to Eva and glimpsed relief on her face. Eva knew he was trying to cut the Rabbi's visit short, for she was anxious to make her views known to him. He hoped she realized there was little they could do, for God in the *Torah* ordered all to "increase and multiply." They knew how serious and observant Joseph was to the *Torah* and so they knew he would quickly agree to the marriage so as to comply with it. All that was left for them to do was to accept the inevitable. They would have to suffer the loss, and as parents, find something else to fill their lives.

"We will speak of this with you later, Rabbi. Shalom Aleichem—Peace be with you."

"Shalom Aleichem," the Rabbi replied as he laboriously stood and walked to the door. "But do not wait too long, for Melcha would make a good wife, and a fine kahlah—daughter-in-law." He looked at Eva, as if he had just seen her. He smiled warmly at her, and bowed slightly. "Shalom, Chava."

"Shalom, Rabbi," Eva blurted, and rushed to the door to open it for him, never taking her eyes off her husband.

"See you on Shabbat—Sabbath," the Rabbi dutifully said, as he once again touched the *mezuzah* on the doorpost, and left the two parents in a mournful contemplation of their impending emptiness.

That Sabbath, Rabbi Delayoh announced to the community in the synagogue, "Yosif bar Yakov is betrothed to Melcha bat Benyamin, and after a year of shiddukhin—engagement—they shall be married."

For ten years, Melcha remained Joseph's faithful wife and a good mother. Like all Jews in their village, their house became the center around which their lives revolved. It was not a splendid house, but like so many others in the town, it was a place of comfort and protection, especially in the winter. Then love seemed to keep all the inhabitants warmer and happier.

Their home was a square two-story dwelling made of clay bricks. These bricks were made of a blend of straw and clay, beaten and pressed by hands and feet and baked in an oven. The single ground-floor room was used as the dining, kitchen and entertainment room. The walls were unadorned except for an occasional wooden shelf which was anchored on the interior wall. There were two windows, covered with heavy curtains when they weren't shuttered. The roof of the house was supported by large heavy wooden beams. There were two doors to the house. The one in the front of the house was wide and tall and on its doorpost was the *mezuzah*, which was to be touched on entering and exiting the house. It contained the *Shema Israel*—the Hebrew prayer of faith. This complied with the *mitzvah*—Bible command—to affix the prayer of faith on the doorpost of every house. The other door, which was at the back of the house, was narrow and low, and led to a small garden and the rest of the property.

The floor was earthen and the four corners in the house were used for family storage and necessities. In one corner, the house dishes, cups, pots, pans and other cooking articles were stored. Water, so exceedingly important to their lives, was stored in skins, jars, jugs or pitchers and usually was in another corner. The storage of flour and food stuff was kept in wooden bins in a third corner. There were also a variety of baskets and bushels used for storage and for carrying of items in the last corner.

Like so many poor Hebrew houses, it contained no fireplace. In good weather, an open fire pit behind the house at some distance was used for cooking. If there was a need for heat in the cold months, small fires were set in a corner of the house with bricks placed around it to contain the flames, cinders and embers. This small fire area was often used to make bread.

The top floor was nothing more than an elevated wooden platform or loft. An inside ladder was used to access this area. The householder stored there the sleeping mats, clothing, linens and whatever finery the family might have.

There was little or no furniture: a few small tables, several stools, a cabinet. Small tables were used to rest things on, and if a larger table was needed for special occasions and holidays, a wooden chest that Joseph had made to store clothing and bedding was used. At most meals, a bushel was turned upside down and all would sit on the floor and eat. The stools, which Joseph had also made, were used to rest on, but most of the time these stools were used for guests and visitors.

The interior of the house was always dark. Daylight was used, and at night a lamp was placed on the floor or hung from the ceiling rafters. Sometimes the lamps were placed on a ledge, or window sill. Olive oil, animal fat, seed oil or vegetable oil was burned in these lamps, which was costly.

The houses were cold in the winter, warm in the summer, and wet in the rain. Often the roof leaked, and the walls dampened when there was a strong rainstorm.

Everyone in the village seemed to have livestock: a donkey, goat, ox, sheep or dog. During the night in the winter months, the livestock was taken indoors, to protect the animals from the winter and hopefully to add some warmth for those in the house.

One of the all–important elements of the house for the everyday Jew was the roof, which was accessible by a staircase on the side of the house. All roofs were slightly slanted to allow rainwater to pour down the wooden gutters that ran along the side of the square houses and emptied into wooden containers or clay jugs. The water was later used for cooking, cleaning and drinking. The washed clothing was left to dry on the roof. In warm weather, the residents would go to the roof to relax and enjoy the evening cool air, often sleeping there at night. Many times in order to have some privacy, the residents of the house would make a tent on the roof. The roof was also used as a place of prayer and meditation.

There was no lavatory in the house. For that detail one had to go out the back door, necessarily a considered distance from the house, and relieve oneself.

Behind every house was a fairly large garden. In gardens like Melcha and Joseph's, leeks, grapes, beets, onions, potatoes, and other vegetables and herbs grew. They even dared to grow a fig tree, which in addition to providing fruit for their table, created shade and another place to relax. Melcha had insisted on growing flowers, and her favorite was the sweet scented jasmine.

In all their years of marriage, Melcha served Joseph as a good wife. She baked bread, ground corn in the small house mill, and cooked meals. She spun, wove and repaired clothing. She washed the family clothes. Every morning she fetched water from the village well for her family needs and to keep the house clean. She led the Sabbath meal and remained a good daughter of the *Torah*. She was a disciplinarian to the children and to her husband but never in public. She stood by Joseph's side in complete obedience, laughed and cried with him when it was necessary. She made him content and bore him three boys and two girls.

One day, she never woke from her sleep and Joseph, as a young man, was a widower with five children.

Joachim walked to the back of his house to his family's little visiting room, and with a loud grunt, sat upon a small stool. He was a tired man, and seemed to be exhausted lately, since his work in the synagogue had changed. His present duties had become more complex and more strenuous, and he was beginning to feel his age. His legs bothered him, as did his back, and he wondered how much longer he would be able to remain at his job. The only thing that kept his short lean body from giving up was his knowledge that what he was doing was the will of God. He strongly believed that what was put before him had to be done correctly and completely. To stop working because of age was contrary to his thinking. As long as he breathed, he had to do something. If God left you on earth breathing, then He expected life and living from you. Joachim momentarily closed his eyes and wondered if he could spend his days at home doing small unimportant things. He wondered if he could remain a good husband to his wife. Surely he would become a burden to her routine by being in her way. They had been married a long time, yet with the children, family, friends constantly around them they rarely were alone. The prospect of being in her company continuously made him uncomfortable. When he opened his eyes, he was surprised to see his wife Anna had quietly entered the room and was gathering clothes to be washed at a later time.

"Hannah—Anna, have you spoken to our daughter Miryam—Mary—about her betrothal?"

"Yes, as you told me to, and I repeat what I said to you before: she needs time."

"Does she need all this time to pick a husband? I should not have listened to you; I should have just picked one for her. What she is doing seems impolite, even disobedient. Why should it be such a big thing to find a good Hebrew man to marry? To keep everyone waiting for her decision is not a good thing." As an afterthought, he continued, "Whoever she picks will be a good husband, because all Hebrew men are good."

"Miryam is not like our older daughter. Shelomit—Salome—knew from the start that Zebediah—Zebedee—was to be her ba'al—husband. Miryam has the need to be careful. She is always careful in all she does; you know that." Anna said, smiling. "Besides, not all Hebrew men are good."

"So say you!" Joachim shot back. "What does she need to be careful about?" His voice rose slightly with impatience. "A husband is one who will tend to her and see that she lives according to the Law. He is a companion in life." He paused, expecting a response, but getting none, he continued: "We grow old and it would be nice to have our youngest daughter married before we die."

"Yehoyakim—Joachim, you grow old, not I." She purposely paused and smiled, knowing her statement was true and that he would be stifled in his argument. "Yet I agree that our daughter should be married before we die. Miryam came too late in our lives and we mellowed and forgot the hard and heavy hand that a young maiden needs. It is not her fault, so let us live with what we have done wrong and be patient."

Joachim grunted and once again closed his eyes.

It is better to leave some things unsaid, he thought. He knew Anna was right. Mary was different from her sister Salome. Salome was quick in her actions; Mary was slow, careful, and less prone to rashness.

Perhaps she is looking for a man such as Zebediah, he thought, inhaling deeply with satisfaction in his son-in-law. Joachim found Zebedee to be respectful, attentive and reliable, and good for his daughter Salome.

Miryam should be so blessed with the likes of Zebediah, he thought. *But Miryam is being too careful and taking too long to make a decision. I grow weary and embarrassed by her delay. Some are thinking I am not the head of my house because of her being so careful.*

Opening his eyes, he said in a more timid tone, "You must talk to her more forcefully, Hannah."

"Yehoyakim," Anna said with exasperation. "Be still. You know as I do that Miryam has dedicated herself to El Shaddai—The Almighty—and that dedication is most important to her. She said she will wait for Him to give her a sign. So it is and so it shall be. Should we go against the wishes of El Shaddai?"

"Maybe obeying the Torah Law is the sign that Miryam should remember," Joachim grunted, and then closed his eyes.

Anna wanted to respond but her response would have put her in danger of offending God. She thought, *So now Yehoyakim, you are saying the Torah is above El Shaddai!*

For several moments the house was silent and Joachim thought he had made his point.

"Ah, Yehoyakim, you are home. Shalom Aleichem."

"Shalom Aleichem, Rabbi Delayoh," Anna replied loudly, knowing this would jolt Joachim to the present.

"Shalom, Hannah." The Rabbi said in a timid voice, with a respectful bow of his head.

Joachim stood immediately when he heard the Rabbi's greeting. He looked at the short aging man with curiosity. The Rabbi saw him every day and a visit from him at home was very unusual. Something must be wrong. He ran through the litany of things and duties that he had done that day to assure himself he had not forgotten anything.

"A cup of cool water, Rabbi?" Anna asked courteously.

"Yes, Hannah, that would be nice, for we have much to talk about."

Oy va'avoy! Oh no! I must have done something to displease him, and he is here to release me of my duties at the synagogue, Joachim thought. His dread of being idle sprang back into his mind.

Anna gracefully walked to the Rabbi and gave him the cup of cool water and stepped away. She watched as the old man drank the water from the cup in courteous short consecutive sips. After seven sips, he lowered the cup and returned it to Anna.

"Thank you, Hannah."

Anna took the cup in both hands, and placed it on a small table nearby. Then she moved to Joachim's side.

The Rabbi cleared his throat and looked at the husband and wife before him. He had known them for many years, and admired their faithfulness to God and to the synagogue. They were both good Israelites.

"Miryam has been to see me. It was nothing serious, but yet, very profound. She told me she had dedicated herself to the will of Adonai—The Lord. She is a very unique young woman. She knows a great deal about the Torah—Five Books of Moses—and the Tanakh—Bible. I was somewhat surprised by her knowledge."

He stopped and looked at them. He knew they had not broken any laws by teaching Mary so much about the Bible, but few females knew all that Mary knew. He was certain that her knowledge had inspired her dedication to God. He waited to see their reaction to his words, and was pleased to observe they did not react in defense or innocence. They had strong convictions.

"She said she learned all she knew about our faith by listening to those around her, and by dwelling on what she had heard. She said she often prayed to Adonai to help her understand Him. She told me she prays often." He cleared his throat, an action that he found very effective to keep people centered on his words. He permitted a few moments to pass and then continued speaking in his slow way, pronouncing every word carefully.

"I am sure she heard much from you for you are good and faithful people. Then she told me of her dilemma: that she could not decide who to marry. She has asked me to give her a way to find the one husband that would please Adonai. She is leaving the choice entirely in His Hands. I thought of this for many hours and have decided that we will comply with her wish and leave it all to Adonai. I have spoken to the three men who have asked for her hand namely, Reuven bar Aharon the soferim—scribe; Shaul bar Chaim the na'alayim—shoemaker; and Yosef bar Yakov the almanah—widower—and nagar—carpenter. I believe they are all good men and any of them would be good for Miryam but with her dedication to Adonai it is best to leave it all to Him. The three men have agreed to meet with me tomorrow and I will give them the method we will follow for Adonai to pick a husband for Miryam. I hope this meets with your approval."

The Rabbi walked to a nearby stool and with a great sigh of agony, slowly lowered himself to sit. This caused Joachim and Anna great discomfort, for they had forgotten their hospitality.

"All this would have been avoided if Yehoyakim had taken a firmer hand and not let Miryam have such freedom."

The Rabbi noticed the look Joachim gave Anna. He suspected that all this was Anna's doing, but Mary was a unique child, so he also believed that had he been Mary's father, he would have been just as lenient as Joachim had been.

"There is no harm. We will proceed as Miryam desires. I will ask all three suitors to leave their mattah—walking staffs—with me. I will place the three staffs on the altar of the sanctuary in the synagogue and leave Adonai to do the rest. If nothing unusual takes place, Miryam will know she must make the choice, but if something happens, then Miryam will be free of having to make the decision. Does this meet with your approval?"

"Yes, Rabbi," they said together.

Joachim sighed silently. Anna smiled, for she knew this is what Mary wanted.

Joseph stood by the window in Joachim's home. He waited impatiently for the arrival of Mary, to whom he was now betrothed. Joachim and Anna sat quietly at the side of the room, trying to be inconspicuous. This was the first official time Joseph and Mary were to see each other after Rabbi Delayoh had announced their expected wedding in the synagogue on the last Sabbath. Joseph was nervous and knew he needed to become calm. He could feel the beads of perspiration forming, and he did not want for this to happen. He did not want to be seen by Mary in an unfavorable light. He did not want her to think anything imperfect or unpleasant about him. He silently wished for a cool breeze.

What is wrong with you, Yosef? he thought. *You are not a stranger to the custom of betrothal. Why are you so unnerved?*

His answer came quickly. He mentally enumerated the extraordinary things that happened during these past few weeks. These happenings seemed to add urgency to this meeting. He had never told anyone of the strong feeling he had that something of great importance was to happen to him through Mary. He had never told anyone of the night that he had rested on his sleeping mat, suspended between sleep and being awake, and had seen Mary walking to him with a lily in her hand and under her feet a carpet of pure white clouds. She had not spoken; she had stood there waiting for him to understand something that could not be put into words. In his stupor, he had waited in confusion, not knowing what to do. He had never seen such a sight. Then from nowhere, he heard a voice say, "She is chosen!" He had awakened completely perplexed.

The next day he worried what the dream—*was it a dream?*—meant. He recollected how Cleopas, his brother, suddenly was overjoyed about his marriage to Mary when before he had been uncertain about it. Cleopas had told Joseph he believed it was the will of

God that Mary was to become his new wife. His own children, who always became disturbed when someone mentioned the idea of their father marrying again, had grown peaceful, almost joyous, when he told them he was thinking of marriage to Mary. Joachim had come to him to speak of the *mohar*—dowry—which, among Israelites, was paid by the groom to the father of the bride. The normal dowry was fifty shekels, but Joachim, knowing Joseph could not afford this amount, agreed to a much lesser sum.

All these unusual things disturbed Joseph so much that he went to Rabbi Delayoh about his observations, and told him that these happenings were beginning to make him feel unworthy of Mary. The Rabbi told him how he had been chosen: that the next day his walking staff which had been left in the synagogue had sprouted a lily. This unnerved Joseph more. In his usual calm way, the Rabbi told him that his feelings were an assurance that God was involved in this union and that Joseph had to learn to accept the will of God. He also said that he did not have to wait the required full year of engagement. He was a widower, and because of that, one month, or at the most, six months, would be his betrothal time. Joseph knew that this exemption was usually extended to widows, but not widowers. Again, customs and attitudes were altered or ignored so that Mary and he could be wed.

He prayed to understand, and another surprise came to him, one he could not explain. His prayer life changed again. He no longer used the Psalms as most Hebrews did when praying, and he no longer spoke to God in his own words. When he prayed now, he had a different feeling inside. He felt that now all he had to do was place himself mentally before God, and remain silent and still. Just being in His Presence seemed to be a prayer. His very life became a period of praise to God. It was as natural as it must have been with Adam in the Garden of Eden—plainly God and Adam—free and unadorned. His prayers were like a silent walk with God, and he felt a deep harmony with Him. There were times that he could almost feel the powerful presence of God by his side, even walking with him. He was certain that this new form of prayer was a gift from God. More importantly Joseph believed that God understood him even when he was not understanding God.

A soft breeze passed Joseph, and he was calmed for a moment. He decided to think no more of these things, for they intimidated him and left him feeling undeserving of this marriage. He resolved to accept what was happening as the will of God. He knew that God was in control of all the things that had happened and would happen to him and Mary. He wanted to be comfortable with this but knew that he was too insistent on needing explanations. Embarrassed by this thought, he relented. He took a deep breath to shore up his courage, and prayed silently.

If, El Shaddai, You wish me to further be Your servant, give me the courage and the strength to be what You want me to be.

Having acknowledged his thoughts to God, his broad shoulders slumped and his chest relaxed. His thoughts returned to Mary. She was not a total stranger to him. He had known her by sight for years. He often saw her going to the village well in the morning hours, and many times he had wished the courage to speak to her, but she always walked with her eyes down and a small, sometimes undetected smile on her face. She walked with simplicity, her steps never disturbing the earth beneath her feet. Her long black hair flowed behind her. Every part of her being projected calm and serenity, so much so that when he saw her, he slipped into complete tranquility. One day as she passed him, he captured the scent of roses. Another time while in the synagogue, he had caught sight of her through the *mechitz*—screen that separated the men from the women, and she looked enraptured. He remembered commenting to himself on how angelic she looked. He was certain that at that moment she stood spiritually in the very presence of God. Remembering these things caused him to take another deep breath, and this once more soothed and calmed him.

Perhaps it was good to think all these things again.

He looked at the heavy gray curtain that separated the two rooms, and him from Mary.

I wonder if Miryam is aware of the many things that have been pushed aside for us to marry.

The curtain was pushed aside and Joseph recognized Salome of Zebedee, Mary's sister, who was all smiles, as she held the curtain for Mary to enter the room. Mary entered as a picture of graciousness. She was wearing a white dress with a brown cord around her waist. The whiteness of the dress accented her tan skin, black hair and dark eyes. She glowed with perfection in her every step. Again as she moved, nothing was disturbed by her steps. The space and air around her embraced her and guided her.

Joseph took one step toward Mary and then stopped. He recognized a difference about her. Her physical beauty was still obvious, but she seemed to have lost her girlish look and looked mature beyond her years. An unfamiliar beauty glowed from within her. It staggered him. He forced himself to gasp for the next breath, and his body shivered. He felt an immensity radiating from her that filled him with great humility.

What has happened that has changed her so?

Mary walked slowly and directly to Joseph. Her eyes were lowered, almost shut, and her head slightly bowed. When she reached him, she stopped and stood silently before him. Slowly she raised her head and eyes.

Her look seemed to search his face. He felt she wanted something from him, something great and something she knew was difficult. He immediately saw a question in her eyes that troubled him. There was a need in her eyes, a glimpse of apprehension, and finally he identified regret. All these perceptions passed through his mind quickly and left him confused and uneasy.

"Miryam," he said, almost as a question.

Perhaps she has realized what I have lived these past months. Perhaps she is as confused and as perplexed as I am.

"Yosef," she replied.

The softness of her voice suddenly calmed his troubled mind and suddenly the question in her eyes became a resolution of something that he needed to know and accept. His entire being seemed to find absolute calmness. Her voice filled him with peace, and yet youth and carefreeness.

"We know you must become acquainted with each other," Joachim said as he abandoned his observation chair, "But we are also here to set a date for the wedding. Rabbi Delayoh anxiously awaits the date we will decide."

"Father," Mary interrupted politely.

"Yes, my child."

"If I may, I would like to speak to Yosef, in private, for few moments."

"Miryam! We…"

"Yehoyakim, please allow Miryam time," Anna interrupted.

Joachim took a deep breath in exasperation. Lowering his head, he slowly walked away from the couple and returned to his observation seat.

Mary turned to Joseph.

"Yosef, I am proud to be your wife, and I am eager to go to your house, but I must ask something of you that is of the upmost importance to me."

"Yes, Miryam, what is it?"

"Can we delay the wedding for a short time? Perhaps two or three months?"

Joseph was surprised and he heard a small sound of disapproval from Joachim and Salome. Anna remained silent.

"I have some news of my elderly cousin, Elisheva Zacharyah—Elizabeth of Zachary, needing me and I must go to her." Mary looked at Joseph, thinking that his moment of thought was a denial, and quickly added, "I would not ask this of you if it were not of the upmost importance to me."

"Of course, Miryam, I would not want in any way to force my will on you." He smiled at her and turned to Joachim and Anna, who approached the couple.

"Miryam, is this really necessary? I have not heard of Elisheva being ill or in any need." Anna caught her daughter by the shoulders and searched her face for a reason.

"Mother, please, this is most urgent. I believe Yosef has agreed."

"But Miryam, this is highly irregular—"

"Yehoyakim, be still. This request is of importance to Miryam. It is her last request of us as her parents and her first of Yosef as her spouse. I think we should remain silent and understand her request," Anna said quietly, though her face showed confusion and concern. She looked at Joseph and smiled faintly. "Yosef, Yehoyakim and I shall accompany Miryam. All will be in order, and she will return to you within the requested time."

"Thank you," Joseph replied. Turning to Mary, he said in an understanding voice, "If this is of that importance, Miryam, then you have my permission, and we shall marry when you return." Again, he caught the scent of roses. The next day, Mary with great haste went to *'Ein Karem*, a city in *Juda*, to the house of Zachary, husband of her distant cousin, Elizabeth.

Joseph walked quickly from the house of Joachim. He had to get away, to distance himself from what he had just witnessed. He tried to race from his own thoughts, that clogged his mind and threw his very being into greater turmoil. A thousand rapid thoughts and questions flashed through his mind from countless directions. They remained unanswered, unreasoned. Like cold icy sentries they froze his mind and left his thoughts and understanding in an empty stagnant place. He squinted his eyes and wrinkled his forehead from a mysterious pain that emanated from deep within his being.

He quickened his steps.

His mind reenacted the moment when he saw Mary, and his mental shout re-echoed in his head: *She is with child! She is with child!*

The shock had hung heavily in the air of the room, and he had looked at Mary with hurt and disappointment.

Her face had reflected a thousand words, but none were spoken—none were permitted to be spoken. Her innocence had been deeply etched on her face in spite of her not so innocent pregnancy. She had held her head high with courage and confidence, yet her eyes had pleaded with Joseph for understanding.

He had heard no explanations, no excuses from anyone. All had waited for him to speak, for him to ask, but no words were spoken, and no questions were voiced. In that room, words and answers could not or would not have made a difference.

She is with child!

Once more he felt his thunderous heartbeat and the sudden rush of warmth to his head and face. He felt the urge to shout and demand an explanation. Again, he rethought the idea to escape, to run instantly from the house of Joachim, to be away.

Once again, he saw the look on Mary's face.

Her eyes pleaded. *For what? Did she expect understanding? Did she really expect me to ignore the obvious? To be sympathetic? To be supportive? How could she think that? How could she?*

He strode faster.

He remembered quickly raising his hand to shield himself from the look in her eye; or did he do that to hide the disgrace from his sight and mind? After that, he had walked briskly from the house and out into the sun. He hurried away, wanting, needing, to put distance between him and the betrayal. He needed to be away from the greatest offense that he had ever lived, an offense that hurt so deeply that he knew it would scar his spirit for many years to come.

How could she?

He walked faster, gasping for air. His head was throbbing. He was growing weak. He had to stop, and when he did, he realized he had walked, possibly run, out of the town of Nazareth and onto one of the nearby hills. Perspiring and weary, he fell to the ground under a shaded tree. Slowly, he started to relax, and his breathing eased, but he was totally exhausted. He did not want to think any longer; he did not want to react. He knew that nothing would ease or make the problem disappear. He had to face his dilemma. He had to decide what to do about his betrothal, his marriage, and about Mary. Everyone knew him, and they knew he would never take advantage of Mary before their wedding. He was not that kind of man. His brother and many others knew that he had no knowledge of her because she had been away for three months, and they never had any chance of knowing each other. The Child she bore was not his. Promptly his mind stopped working, and the feeling of betrayal pressed heavily on him. It pushed against him from all sides, causing him to think of only one thing: he had to end this marriage.

He had been duped. He wondered if, in his innocence and in his desire, that all the surprising events had been more of his own imagination than the will of God.

Have I fooled myself? How brazen I was to assume that El Shaddai had planned all these conveniences.

In complete aloneness, his mind became filled with empty spaces that could not be filled by words or thinking. He was drained. He grew sad, feeling unwanted and dejected. He swiftly found comfort in self-pity. He was the blind and stupid fool in this farce, in this tragedy. He closed his eyes tightly and let the feeling of pity swell within him. When he could not stand it any longer, he broke off his thinking and returned to the urgency of a solution.

The whole thing was a mistake. Miryam really wanted one of the other suitors and I was chosen by mistake. All that happened to make things smooth were in my imagination. I wanted all to be perfect, for I was the least worthy. I duped myself. No doubt one of the others is the father of the Child. Her trip to visit her cousin was only a ploy to meet her choice. No matter! For now I see El Shaddai has spoken His will. It is not my trumped-up idea of what was to be, but His will. So be it. He took a deep breath and exhaled. *From this day on I shall become more of a listener of the will of El Shaddai than a thinker.*

He closed his eyes and made the resolution penetrate his mind. A few moments passed and then he forced his mind to grown blank.

No more thoughts or words, I must act. I must end this immediately.

The night was deep in darkness. It was the coldest of any night he had ever lived. The blackness filled his mind and the night chill clung to his bones. Everything about that night was heavy and thick. He envisioned himself standing perilously on a bleak cliff of a dark mountain with anguish all around him. Lying on his sleeping mat, he could not sleep. His thoughts were with Mary. He knew that to reveal her disgrace would bring her and her family much shame, and he did not want to cause anyone that much pain. He knew he could not allow her to be put to death by stoning. The very thought caused him to shiver and grow even colder. He could not send her to that fate.

I will quietly, yes very quietly, "put her away" and that will be it. Yehoyakim and Hannah will quietly send Miryam back to her cousin to have the Child in secrecy. There will be no disgrace on her. I am a widower and no one will think badly of her. They will think I still mourn my wife and cannot find another to take her place. And when my family asks me I shall tell them that Melcha is still in my mind and heart.

He stopped for a moment and the thought of his first wife slowly spread over him.

It would not be a lie, for often, still, she holds my heart.

A small satisfied smile came across his lips. She had been his first love. He would never love another or marry again.

One love in a lifetime is all that a man should receive, he thought. *I have had my allotted one and my allotted time.*

He lingered there in the happy thoughts of his life with his first wife. Moments later, his mind returned to the resolution of Mary. He was pleased. He was certain that he had settled his dilemma with dignity and fairness to Mary, her family and himself. A warm peace came over his mind and he grew satisfied.

Unexpectedly, several questions sprung into his mind in quick succession: *And what of El Shaddai? How am I to reconcile this with Him? Is my proposed deception pleasing to Him?*

He sat up on his sleeping mat and looked into the darkness. It was a good place to speak to his unseen God.

El Shaddai, You must see the dilemma I am in. I have to lie or pretend that I have no need for Miryam. I have to do this, for I cannot allow her to be harmed. I do not think You would want me to harm any of Your creatures. You will have to find forgiveness in my heart, for I have very few choices here. I thought You had Your hand in this marriage, but it seems I was only hoping and pushing for the exceptions to be a confirmation of Your will. Perhaps my presumption is the fault in this marriage; perhaps this is Your way of making me humble and not so much like my ancestors. If what I am about to do is not pleasing to You, then I am sure You will stop it. I place it all in Your hands.

Satisfied he returned to his mat and rested. Closing his eyes he uttered a soft, low thanks to God. He relaxed his body as he felt a great heaviness lift from him.

Tomorrow, life will be better, and a new meaning to life will be discovered with the help and will of El Shaddai, he thought.

Slowly, like the gentle, harmless and welcome rise of cool water, peace came over his burning and tormented mind. Sleep slipped over him and he slept.

He dreamed.

He was walking on a road. It was not a dirt road like the many around Nazareth. It was a Roman road, yet like none other he had ever seen. Roman roads were constructed with the greatest of care. He felt it a great honor to be a traveler on a road such as this. Ahead, the road continued endlessly, to a far destination. There were no hills on the side of the road. The land was flat and green, with grass that spread far into the distance, until it reached the beginning of the soft light-blue sky. He had never seen land like this.

As he walked, he looked at the stonework beneath his bare feet, and wondered why the rough surface was not causing him discomfort. He thrust his staff on the granite and was surprised that his staff made no sound. These things troubled him momentarily, but he soon forgot these trivialities because of the comfort he felt on this road, in the certainty that this road was made for and belonged to him and him alone. He acknowledged the privilege of walking this road, and recognized the blessing that was reserved only for him. A soft and pleasant breeze pressed against him, and slowly slipped through him, bringing refreshment.

Unexpectedly, he found a man in a white garment walking by his side.

"Shalom alekhem—peace to you, my fellow traveler," the stranger said, with a wide smile.

"Shalom," Joseph replied politely, though his mind was stinging with surprise and curiosity at the stranger's sudden appearance.

"It is a good day to walk. I find whenever I need to think clearly, a good walk is a great thing to do. Do you not agree, Yosef?"

"How did you know my name?"

"You look like a Yosef," the stranger replied. "Apparently I am right, but please do not be bothered. I have always guessed people's names correctly. It is a gift from on High."

Joseph turned away from the stranger and looked at the road ahead. He wondered where this road would take him. It was a long straight road that seemed to go on and on.

All roads have to have an end, he thought.

"Roads end only when the traveler has completed his walk," the stranger said.

Joseph snapped his head quickly to view the man, and said with some amusement, "Sir, you seem to have uncommon talents. You read thoughts as well as know the names of strangers?"

"When I need to. I will stop if you feel I am intruding."

"No, I just find it unusual. I am somewhat envious of your gifts."

"There will be days on which you will be given gifts; you will be made wiser than many others, for you will hear, see, and understand many hidden things. There will be other days ahead that will be hidden from you to spare you sorrow, but you still shall feel the burden."

"So, sir, you are a prophet as well as a reader of minds and knower of names?"

"No, I am only what I am needed to be."

"Stranger, you speak in riddles, yet you fascinate me," Joseph said lightly.

"You call me Stranger; now I am the one fascinated."

"Well I do not know you, so you are a stranger to me. But apparently I am not a stranger to you, for you know things about me."

"Yosef, I know many things about you. I know your mother Chava and your father, Yakov."

"Oh, Stranger," Joseph said, chuckling, "That seems near impossible, for you cannot be old enough to have known my parents. They died many years ago and you are still a young man."

"I know them," the stranger said emphatically. "I know your wife Melcha. You missed her greatly tonight and acknowledged it, only momentarily."

Joseph stopped walking and looked at the stranger, but the stranger quickly reached for Joseph's arm. With a small pull, he encouraged him to continue to walk.

"You cannot stop on this road, or on this journey. You must always go forward. Forward is the future, and the future moves us all to the end."

Joseph chuckled to himself. "Again a riddle! Who are you?"

"I am a Malach."

"Your name means 'messenger,'" Joseph said casually.

Now the stranger chuckled.

"Yes, Yosef, it means 'messenger'. Sometimes it means more, but that does not matter. And your name, Yosef, means 'He will increase.' The Holy One must have great things in store for you. It appears He wants you to add to His world. What I see and know of you in our short walk makes me guess you will add much to His Word and to His creation."

"I doubt that, sir. I believe El Shaddai thinks I am a pompous old, yet young, man who thought life was to begin anew for him, and that everything was made easy for him."

"You call him El Shaddai, I…we call Him 'Hakkadosh Barukh Hu'—The Holy One Blessed be He."

The two continued to walk the road in silence.

"I do not believe 'The Holy One Blessed be He' thinks of you as a pompous young man. I am sure He sees you as His son. He has blessed you with good and holy parents, with Melcha—a devoted and loving wife, and now with Miryam as your new wife."

"You speak correctly, Malach, about my departed parents and wife, but I am not taking Miryam as a wife."

"Why not? Do you think you are not worthy to be the father of the Child?"

"How do you know these things, Sir?" Joseph said, then regretted having confirmed Mary's motherhood by his startled reply.

Suddenly, Joseph was embraced by a heavy stillness, yet he knew he was still moving. He knew he could not stop for he was being moved by something outside himself. His body was being taken over and he was willing to allow this to happen. Silence and peace simultaneously held him in total tenderness. He felt himself being lifted and taken to a place of great enormity.

"Yosef!"

The voice Joseph heard was full of authority and demanded immediate respect. It was not the voice of the stranger. He turned to look at his companion and saw Malach surrounded by a bright white radiance that yet did not hurt his eyes.

Malach slowly rose above Joseph and with a new voice said, "Yosef bar Duhvid, fear not to take unto thee Miryam as thy wife, for that which is conceived in her, is of the Ruach Hako'desh—Holy Spirit. And she shall bring forth a Son, and thou shalt call His name Yeshu'a—Jesus, for He shall save His people from their sins."

A strong wind pushed against Joseph and suddenly he found himself alone on the endless road. In all the time that Malach had been speaking, he had not traveled far. He became conscious of the tap of his staff against the granite and his feet suffering from the roughness of the stone. He was pleased and relieved by what had been told to him. He thought of Mary with profound respect, and unexpectedly around him he smelled the scent of roses, though there were no rose bushes in sight.

He woke from his dream and spent the rest of the night waiting for the dawn and his trip to Joachim's house, and Mary.

He walked as quickly as he could. He had a mandate from Heaven. There was no doubt in his mind that this was the will of God, and that God had entrusted this task to him and him alone. In the back of his mind he thought that he was now part of the Ancient Ones—the Prophets and Judges, yes, and maybe the Kings of Israel—who had been called and ordered by God to perform duties for Him. This did not make Joseph proud, instead it humbled him and made him feel privileged and eager to serve. He moved and lived out of faith: complete raw faith. No questions asked, no knowledge of God's plan needed. He had been called to do, and that was all he needed to know.

When Joseph arrived at Joachim's house, he was met at the door by Anna, Mary's mother. Her face was wrinkled from time and concern. Her eyes were red from lack of sleep and undoubtedly from tears. Her short thin body slumped and looked beaten. Her round face was heavy with concern and sadness. Her brown hair, sprinkled with white, was carelessly covered by a veil.

"Yosef, come." Her words were a plea, not a command, and Joseph obediently followed her around the side of the house to the small stable attached to the house.

When they arrived in the stable, Anna quickly turned and looked directly at Joseph.

"Yosef, what I am about to tell you is most difficult. You must listen carefully to me. I know how you must feel, how betrayed and used you feel, and I know that you are within your right to denounce Miryam, but before you do anything you must hear what I have to say, and know what I have witnessed."

"It is all fine, Hannah, I have…"

"No!" This time her voice was a command, then with a mixture of apology and warmth in her eyes she said softly, "Please…listen."

Joseph nodded only because the old woman looked on the verge of collapsing. Fearing that she was growing faint, he looked around the stable for a place for her to sit. Seeing a bale of straw nearby, he gently guided her to it.

"My heart ached for you yesterday when you saw that Miryam was with child. I wanted to scream at you the information I knew. I had spoken to her and told her that she must explain all to you, but she said it was not for her to say. She said that your knowing was in the Hands of El Shaddai. This did not sit well with me, so all night I prayed for guidance, and by this morning I believed that I should tell you what I saw, and hope you will understand."

She stopped and searched Joseph's eyes for a flicker of understanding or sympathy, but she did not see any. He seemed distant and preoccupied with other thoughts.

With quick excited words, she rattled on: "As we traveled to my cousin Elisheva's house, Miryam informed us that she had received word from an angel that my cousin was with child. Yehoyakim and I laughed. Elisheva was old and past the time for her to bear a child; she has been barren all her life. Miryam insisted, so we thought it wise to let her believe what she wanted to believe. The idea of an angel giving her this information was impossible, for the pregnancy of my cousin was most unbelievable. When we arrived at my cousin's house, Miryam called out Elisheva's name in a loud voice. My cousin came out of the house and stood by the portals."

Anna stopped. She swallowed hard for the words she wanted to speak struggled to be voiced.

"Elisheva was—was—with child! How could this be? My mind went blank and I almost turned into a pillar of salt. My eyes were witnessing a miracle and they filled with tears of joy, for I knew how she had longed to be a mother."

Shaking her head in disbelief, she continued: "Elisheva quickly laid her hand on her stomach, as if to calm a disturbance or affirm an action. She saluted Miryam by crying out in a loud voice: 'Blessed art thou among women, and blessed is the Fruit of thy womb. And whence is this to me that the mother of my Lord shall come to me? For behold, as soon as the voice of thy salutation sounded in my ears, the infant in my womb leaped with joy.'"

"I rushed to my cousin and embraced her with great happiness. I was still in shock at what I had witnessed. Sometime later when things were calmer, I heard Elisheva's voice and words again and I shivered. I quickly went to Miryam and asked her, 'What matter of greeting was this—"the mother of my Lord"?' And she told me of an angel telling her she was to bear a Child."

Anna's voice trailed off, for Joseph's mind had gone to another place. He was a man of determination; he had a mission to perform. He had not heard what Anna was saying. He knew her concerns for her daughter, and he let this thought lead him to appear to be listening to her.

Unexpectedly, Joseph saw the face of Mary before him on the day she asked permission to go see her cousin Elizabeth. Again he saw the question on her face and the need in her eyes. Then he heard the Angel Malach's voice, "You will be made wiser than many others for you will hear, know, see and understand many hidden things."

He became aware of the silence between him and Anna. He smiled, not in agreement with what she had said, for he had not heard, but from politeness to show understanding. He then told Anna of his nighttime visitor and his intent to marry Mary.

"All that you say means little for I must do what is needed of me." With these words, he turned and went back to the house of Joachim to see his new bride.

They set the date and prepared for the wedding, following the customs of marriage according to the traditions of their people.

Every time he saw Mary, Joseph grew more concerned about her and more impressed with her plain beauty. Her true exquisiteness was not visible: it was deep within her and she carried it with simplicity. The brilliance that shone from her was wrapped in pure innocence. Joseph saw her as fragile and so young, yet paradoxically she showed signs of great strength and maturity beyond her years. As time passed he saw great knowledge in her eyes that made him feel that she knew many mysteries. He suspected that she had wisdom that came from history, not just the history of the Jewish people, but of all people. He observed her entire being change with each passing day; and she glowed more as her time grew near. In her presence he sensed a great spirituality, one so great that he longed to possess some of it. Her nobility, a peasant nobility, was covered in humility so great that even humbleness blushed. He could understand why she had been chosen to do this important thing for God.

The miracle of life within her body amazed Joseph. Conception was always a miracle to him but conception from the command of God astonished him even more. God had once again entered the theater of mankind. He once again had spoken a Word and it was done and surely He found it to be good. This was an overwhelming thought to Joseph, making him grow weak as he tried to grasp and understand it.

After they married, Joseph wanted to take Mary away from the questioning eyes of the Nazarenes. He thought of returning to Bethlehem to be among his relatives there but he and Mary could not take such a journey alone. It was far too dangerous. So Mary remained in seclusion at the insistence of her husband and her parents. This seclusion was customary for pregnant Jewish women, so the tradition was a convenience for them. Few in their families knew of her pregnancy and if they had known, Joseph was certain they would have agreed to Mary's isolation.

During this time Joseph continued to work in his small carpenter shop and found new enthusiasm for his work. Woodworking was in his blood. His father, his grandfather, and his great-grandfather, were carpenters. As far back as the family could remember, wood had been in their lives, yet for reasons he could not explain, now wood had become a different and all-encompassing thing. There was a new calmness and contentment that settled over him, a welcome relief after all these months of stress, turmoil and mind straining decisions. The world seemed normal, and moved without notice around Mary and himself.

He believed that their lives would be this way forever. Why wouldn't it? Mary and he had been asked to be a part of a great unknown plan of God. This Child would have a special relationship with God, and Joseph was certain that Mary and he would also have God's protection for they were doing His will. Although the rest of the plan was a mystery to Joseph, he did not need to know. Knowing that God knew and the Child knew was enough for him. Unexpectedly, he felt curious; he wanted to smother the thought, kill it before it bloomed, but he fell to weakness and let it come into being.

Truly, he thought, *El Shaddai will give us some special blessings. We will not expect riches or great positions, only a degree of comfort and ease.* The thought created a sour taste in his mouth and he almost became physically ill. *Yosef, you and Miryam are doing the will of El Shaddai, how could you expect earthly reward for doing what is asked of you when He has done so much for you?*

He quickly turned away, as if to reject himself and the very space that he had occupied when this thought had life.

El Shaddai, please forgive me. I am but a human and weak man. I am made of the same cloth of Adam. I, like Moses, forgot what You have done for us…for me. Please, I beg You to forgive my weakness and my stupidity. Why You chose me to do Your will I will never know or understand. You know I was not the best choice or the wisest, yet it fell to me. Help me to find the humility of a true servant and not be the stiff-necked human being I have become through habit and ancestry. Help me to be more like Miryam.

Swiftly an image of Mary came to his mind's eye and he began to deflate. He slowly crumbled to the floor. She was an example and he had failed again to see her as such. For the first time in his life he felt unworthy of being a member of the Chosen People. He had failed to acknowledge the greatness of his spouse; he had failed to rely on her humility and faith. His eyes watered from shame.

El Shaddai, help me to know what it is I am to be. Help me know what I am to do. Grant me Your blessings so I may do only Your Holy Will. Help me to keep my will out of the workings You have in mind. I am a ship without a sail; I have no directions. All I have are the words of Malach: they gave a command and I obeyed, but I do not know for what purpose. If it is not for me to know, rid me of my curiosity and confusion and guide me to blind obedience.

His mind went blank; the room was still, silent. After many long moments, Joseph laboriously rose from the floor, seeking the support of his wooden work table to stand. He knew there would be no answer, but he was equally certain that in God's time he would know all that was his to know. Satisfied with this conclusion, he relaxed. He was happy that he had made known his thoughts to God. Slowly he began gathering his tools to return to work.

We sometimes must find the answers to our own prayers, he thought. *That is why we have free thought.*

He returned to his wood cutting. Perhaps knowing all of God's will was too dangerous for a mortal such as he. Maybe God was protecting him. He immediately uttered a prayer of thanksgiving.

I wonder if Miryam knows what this Child will be and what He is to do for our people. Perhaps her angel told her more than I was told. I am certain: she must have been told more. All Malach the angel said to me was "…He shall save His people from their sins."

Joseph stood erect. He squared his shoulders and his chest expanded with a deep breath of pride and freedom. His eyebrows lifted. A small smile widened his mouth and he began to wonder if he had found the reason for the Child being sent by God. He quickly offered a prayer of praise and thanksgiving to God.

If He is to save His people from their sins, as Malach said, then He would have to be a religious teacher—a holy one. A Rabbi? A great Rabbi, who will show our people new meanings of the Torah? Of course, Yosef, you are such a fool, he told himself. *You had the answer before you. It was given to you by El Shaddai and your angel, but you did not see, hear or understand. You must make all your senses keen. You know El Shaddai speaks in roundabout ways.*

His smile widened to reveal his even teeth. He inflated his lungs with satisfaction, for he felt God's closeness. He was no longer in the darkness, feeling neglected. He basked in this joy for several moments and finally reached for his mallet. He must stop day-dreaming and return to work.

He was making a small wooden stool for Rabbi Delayoh's wife. The Rabbi wanted the stool in two days to give as a gift, and Joseph had to finish it before he left for Bethlehem. He was so deeply engrossed in his work that he failed to hear his brother Cleopas enter the small shop.

"Yosef, we have purchased the oxen and the mules. The carts are finished and in a few hours we will begin packing for our trip. My wife tells me that you are not ready to leave. You know that we must be in this cara-van for Bethlehem for the census. You also know that we must hurry in order to get lodging in the City of David. If we wait too long, we may find ourselves trav-eling during the Shabbath and this will delay us more for we would have to stop and observe the Holy Day."

"Chaleph—Cleopas, I hurry. I have promised this stool for Rabbi Delayoh and I must have it ready for him. I still have a half-day's work on it. Please do not rush me for I may become too anxious and fail to do good work. I assure you that my wife and I will be ready in a day's time. All the children are ready and excited to leave and I know they have been packed for days."

"Yosef, your wife is near her time; the longer you delay the closer you put her to her date."

"El Shaddai will provide for all things, Chaleph. Learn this and you will be at peace."

"Yosef, you amaze me. My wife worries, Miryam's parents—Hannah and Yehoyakim—worry, Shelomet—Miryam's sister—worries, and you and your wife say 'El Shaddai will provide.' Sometimes your understanding of what El Shaddai has in store amazes me; it seems like you have some special connection. I pray someday to be like you both and have the understanding of Him as you do."

Joseph smiled. He stopped working to look at his brother. "Someday, brother, El Shaddai will use you if you open your heart to His Will."

"When that happens I pray I shall be as certain as you are. But until that day, I suggest you hurry with your task and be ready to leave early tomorrow and not a full day from now. The rest of us shall not wait any longer for you. If we do not leave as a family group, you and Miryam will have no one to travel with." Cleopas turned and walked out of the shop, hoping he had put fear in his brother's heart. He touched the *mezuzah* on the portal, and without looking back, repeated, "Early tomorrow, Yosef."

Joseph smiled. *He's a worrier. That is why his hair is graying before its time and he looks more like my father than my brother.* He smiled, then chuckled. *Most of the time, he even acts like my father.*

He returned to his work, knowing that God would move the world and life at His time and pace.

The next day, Cleopas and his wife Mary and their children; Joseph and his pregnant wife, Mary, and his children from his first marriage assembled. Before beginning the walk to Bethlehem for the census of the Emperor Caesar Augustus and Quirinius the Governor of Syria, they prayed:

"Yehi ratzon milefanecha Adonai Eloheinu veilohei avoseinu…

May it be Your will, Lord, our Lord and the Lord

of our fathers, that You should lead us in peace and

direct our steps in peace, and guide us in peace,

and support us in peace, and cause us to reach our

destination in life, joy, and peace. Amen."

The journey from Nazareth to Bethlehem took four or five days. The more direct route took them south across the *Emek Yizrael*—Jezreel Valley—and through the Hill Country of *Shomron*—Samaria. This was a physically demanding route, for the hilly country and many valleys made travel difficult. The land was a place of deep silence, hot and dry, and at night bone-chilling. It was an untamed yet dramatically beautiful land. The constant ascent and descent of the mountainous land would affect Mary, who suddenly was showing signs of nearing the end of her pregnancy.

That route would take the caravan through Samaria, where there would be no lodging or compassion from the inhabitants because of the hostilities and "no dealings" policy that existed between Jews and Samaritans.

So Cleopas and Joseph decided to take the alternate route, southeast to the Jezreel Valley. They would cross the *Hay Yarden*—Jordan River, which flowed parallel to the valley, and travel along the east bank until they by-passed Samaria. They would follow the river valley through Decapolis and Perea. They would cross back over the Jordan River and be in the region of *Yehuda*—Judea. They would continue west to Bethphage and Bethany where they had some distant relatives, and then south to Bethlehem. This route would give them a continual supply of river water for their families, the mules that carried their supplies, and the oxen that pulled their carts. They were assured of good lodging with the comfort and hospitality of friendlier people, and because the Jordan Valley was below sea level the constant daily temperature was pleasant and mild.

One hundred people composed the caravan, mostly men. This gave everyone a feeling of security against the robbers and bandits who roamed the wilderness.

Cleopas and Joseph expected the children and the women, especially Mary, to grow tired from the long walk, so they had purchased and repaired two old wooden carts. These carts, drawn by oxen, were a refuge for the tired. Three mules carried supplies. Several nights they lodged with generous Jews, and other nights they built a lean-to and slept outdoors. The journey was uneventful, and as comfortable as could be expected.

When they reached *Yenho*—Jericho, Mary became very uncomfortable. It was decided that both families would wait a day until she was fit to travel. After a day's delay, they traveled to Bethphage and Bethany. Again Mary began having some discomfort, so they waited. After two nights, Cleopas, his family and Joseph's children went on to Bethlehem to find lodging, leaving Mary and Joseph behind to have more time to recuperate. After three days and three nights, Joseph and Mary continued their six-mile journey toward Bethlehem. They hurried, for the time of the census taking was drawing to a close and her time was near.

Bethlehem was a small village in Judea of about fifteen acres, so small that it had no wall around its boundaries to defend it from invaders. In Judea, only towns had walls to defend the populace, distinguishing the villages from the towns. The people of Bethlehem were mostly poor farmers or shepherds. Bethlehem had a history far greater than many towns and other communities in Judea. Its name means "house of bread." It was often called *Ephrathah*, and had been identified as the burial place of Rachel, the favorite wife of Jacob. The village was founded by Caleb's son Salma, the "father" of Bethlehem. The beautiful story in *Megilath Ruth*—the Scroll of Ruth, of Naomi, Ruth and Boaz, David's great-grandparents, is set in and around Bethlehem. David was raised in this village, and it was called the "City of David." Here the Prophet Samuel anointed David king over Israel. The Prophet Micah prophesied that from this village "a ruler of Israel will come." Bethlehem had been marked for future history and greatness.

As Joseph and Mary approached the outer limits of Bethlehem, they felt the chill of the night. High above them was the open sky with its million stars. The moon was full, reflecting onto the land and giving it a gray-blue hue. The silent and empty land that surrounded the small village gave Bethlehem a singleness that always conveyed a feeling of utter aloneness and independence. Joseph acknowledged an unwelcoming air the village.

As they came into the crowded village, the noise and clamor was all around them. The couple felt isolated. It was not what Joseph had expected, and he felt disheartened.

But as they advanced, Joseph began cheerfully pointing out the places that were still familiar to him. Mary watched him as a parent watches a child showing off and showing an adult around his play area. She smiled at his youthful excitement. After each discovery he had a story of someone or something associated with that place or thing.

Finally, Joseph realized that he was being selfish for not finding lodging for her right away. He abruptly stopped his rambling and led their donkey in the direction of the house of his uncle Gavrie, his father's brother. He was disappointed to discover that there was no room for them in the house. His uncle's family had grown greatly and with all his sons and their wives and grandchildren's wives, husbands, and families, there was no room. A few amicable sentences were exchanged with promises to see his relatives later. Joseph quickly dismissed his disappointment and led the mule to the house of Melek, his mother's brother. Again he found there was no room for them. Joseph was growing concerned, and he wondered what was wrong. He decided to try his cousin Aaron's house. He had not gone there first because he knew that Cleopas and his family and own children were lodging there.

"Stay well, Miryam, I am sure that brother Chaleph has made provision for us at my cousin's house." He hoped to ease her distress, but knew they would be overcrowded too. "Soon we will arrive and all will be well."

"I have prayed, and I am sure all will be well. El Shaddai will provide." She sighed deeply. The sigh alarmed Joseph and he rushed to her side. "I am well, Yosef. I do not mean to be troublesome or a burden, but I think my time grows very near."

Joseph hurried across the village to his cousin's house, but when they arrived, again, there was no room. Even Cleopas was not lodged there. He was told that Cleopas and his family were at an inn. He returned to Mary with the bad news.

"There are two inns in Bethlehem; I will try them," he said. Without waiting for Mary to answer him, he jerked the donkey's reins to move the animal more quickly behind him. He continued his walk in silence. His head was low as he fought back tears of frustration. He smothered the urge to shout in anger at the inhabitants of Bethlehem that a great Rabbi was on the verge of coming to them, and they had made no room for Him.

If I have failed You, El Shaddai, forgive me. I have done all I could do. It seems I have failed, for I am unable to do the simple job of finding a proper resting place for the child. But if You do not mind and You have willed this to be so, then whatever we find for lodgings will be accepted. I do not know how things went wrong. This journey was so carefully planned, yet things have not gone perfectly. Perhaps we should have departed earlier and thereby have been assured of lodging, but I was doing Your will by making the stool for the Rabbi.

He stopped thinking for a moment and reviewed their dilemma.

How am I to do anything for You and the Child You have sent if I cannot do this simple task? What am I to be in this family? This is the most basic duty of a father—to provide shelter for his family—and I could not do this simple thing. Of what value am I, El Shaddai? I humbly beg You to help me in this endeavor. Perhaps caring for this Child of Yours is too great a duty for me. Help me to be worthy of the task You have set for me.

Joseph looked back at Mary and saw the look of solace and peace on her face, and from her he drew comfort.

She has the hardest burden. When the Babe is born things will become better, for then El Shaddai will speak to us and tell us what we must do. Things will get better; I firmly believe that.

At the first inn, Mary asked Joseph to help her from the donkey and he did. Together they went inside. People were sitting on the floor; some slept on sleeping mats, others milled around the crowded room stepping over those on the floor. Many glared at the two new people at the portal. The inn reeked of unwashed bodies and clothing and cooked food. Even the smell of animals was in the air and Mary quickly covered her mouth. Joseph wrapped his arm around her to give her courage and consolation.

The innkeeper, on seeing them at the door, approached. He looked angry, almost belligerent, but when he saw Mary, his expression changed to deep sympathy.

"I know you are looking for lodging, but as you can see I have no room at all. I have not had any room for days. I am so sorry."

Joseph's heart sank and he turned to Mary in complete desperation. One glance and he knew.

"Yosef…" Mary said.

Joseph turned to the innkeeper.

"Sir, please, have you any shelter?" he asked urgently. "I think her time is too close for us to go on looking for lodging."

"There is a small cave next to the inn," the Innkeeper replied. "We sometimes use it as a stable. It is the only thing I can offer you; and I think you should take it for your woman looks like she is about to become a mother."

"Directions please, sir."

Following the keeper's directions, they rushed to the stable on the side of the inn. A small fence across the entrance of the cave secured the few animals inside. A few of the wooden slats were missing and others hung loosely from the fence. Small hills of hay were strewn around the cave. In a dark corner of the stable, a cow and an ox stood. A few hens scurried about. The cave reeked from animal urine and excrement.

Joseph removed his cloak and threw it on one of the small hills of hay. He tenderly escorted Mary to it so she could rest. As she sat, a sigh escaped her lips. Joseph went to the donkey and unloaded the provisions they had, and then led the donkey into the cave and placed him with the other animals.

"Are you feeling well, Miryam?"

"I am fine, Yosef, just a bit tired."

"If you are well, then I shall get some wood and build a small fire for light and warmth."

He stopped and looked around the cave. A smile crossed his face and he said, "Miryam, when I was a child I used to play in this cave and with the animals housed here. Who would have thought that one day I would return here to find lodging? Who would have believed that in this place of cold, dampness and stench, El Shaddai would fulfill His will?"

He sighed, and returned to the small amount of food, blankets and other provisions they had taken with them. As he arranged them, he became embarrassed as he assessed the cave and the inadequacy of it.

Obviously my expectation of grandeur was premature. El Shaddai is teaching me a lesson. I need to stop being Yosef bar Yakov and become Yosef bar El Shaddai. I must be a father to His messenger and become a servant to Him. I must become like the elders in our history and be a true servant of El Shaddai. You will have to help me, El Shaddai. Please give me the power to do that which You want of me. I am not asking to become perfect, but make me adequate in Your eyes and acceptable to Miryam.

He turned to leave the cave to search for firewood.

"Yosef, before you leave, promise me you will not feel that you have failed El Shaddai. Let us always remember that what happens to us and to this Child is His will. We are only channels in which His will shall be manifested. This Child wants and needs to be born in obscurity rather than greatness and pomp. El Shaddai, I think, wanted this birth to be quiet and unknown and overlooked. We are to record His birth but not proclaim it or declare it. All will be done in the way and in the time of El Shaddai."

Joseph looked at Mary in amazement. Her ability to know what he felt and thought and her complete understanding of what was to happen in their lives left him speechless and humble.

"Miryam, you are so wise, and far better prepared for what is ahead of us. I am still confused and unsure of my part in this plan of El Shaddai. I need you to help me, to guide me and teach me to understand what is expected of me. Help me to learn what to do with my manly thoughts and my human frailties. Forgive me, if I be too human in my new duty. I have been a father and as such, I was able to control events, but with this Child I feel that nothing is in my hands. All is planned and predestined and I am only to fulfill my part."

Mary looked at Joseph with sympathy. She smiled meekly and said, "I am as you are. I also am without any special directions, but I know that I am to bear what I am to bear and to rely on El Shaddai. We shall learn together, and together we shall be taught. Now, go gather wood for the fire that will give us the light we need and the warmth El Shaddai wants us to have."

With great humility and peace, and greater love, Joseph left to do his chore. He walked around the area near the stable, and by the light of the full moon was able to see fallen tree branches and broken bushes. He was happy to be able to gather so many for his fire, but suddenly became disheartened.

How sad it is for me to be looking for dead, unwanted, discarded, broken pieces of creation for this Child. It does not seem proper for a Chosen Messenger of El Shaddai. Again I am confused by Your will, and yet I find Miryam's words reassuring, that all that is taking place is Your will. I should have come to this conclusion myself but I am a man who does things. A man who makes things from destroyed wood. I am a man of conclusions and exactness. He shook his head. *I must learn, as Miryam has said, and leave all to faith.* He smiled to himself. *El Shaddai, you know if I did not act like a stiff-necked Israelite, I would not be a true Israelite. Help me to break the mold, so that I may become the first new Israelite.*

Aloud he said, "This Child should have light, miraculous light, guiding Him to us. This Child should have thunder rumbling across the land and lightning slicing across the night sky. There should be dancing in the villages and people gathering, singing His praises and giving Him the honor due Him." He paused. "This is what I wish I could give Him, but He is not mine, so what You will, so shall it be."

Having gathered all the wood he thought he would need, he began his return to the stable. As he neared their poor lodgings, he saw a bright white light radiating from within and he knew that the miracle had happened. In the distance he heard singing but his mind did not completely acknowledge what he heard. His heart beat rapidly. He stopped, and for an instant he hesitated. He did not know what to expect.

How will this Child look? What am I to say or do for One who came into being by the Word of God?

Then his thoughts went to Mary and he quickened his steps for he believed she must be in need of him.

When he arrived at the opening of the stable, he peeked childishly inside, his arms still holding the abandoned wood. He saw Mary. Her face was aglow. Light radiated from her and the Child. There was no need for his wood to light the stable or warm the stable, for there was both light and warmth blazing from within it. The Babe lay in the fold of Mary's arms within her cloak and covered with further warmth by Joseph's cloak. "Miryam, is all well?"

"Oh yes, Yosef." She looked at him with wonder and awe. "It just happened."

"Do you need anything? Can I do something for you?" he asked. With nothing else to do, he busied himself piling the wood and starting a fire.

The former cave became a home with all its comforts and love. It was now a place of great joy and beauty. A new fragrance filled the air. The sound of angelic voices singing soft cradlesongs and choruses and serenades made the night become a new day. Even the animals, whose shadows softly grayed the back of the cave, stood watching with glazed eyes.

The animals seem to understand what this hour means, Joseph thought to himself.

After he had finished, Mary asked him to help her with the strips of cloth her mother had given her to swaddle the Child. When she had finished, she cuddled the Babe in her arms again and rewrapped Him in Joseph's cloak.

Joseph forced himself to find things to do. He knew he had not looked at the Child nor had he in any way acknowledged Him. He did not know what to do. He felt out of place.

What am I to do? What am I to say? What is the proper way to acknowledge this Child—this special being from God? I am most unworthy to gaze upon a direct messenger of El Shaddai. How do I speak to One Who is so superior to me?

"Yosef, look at the Babe," Mary said.

Slowly, with the beats of his heart becoming as one beat, he turned. His legs buckled and he was on his knees. His eyes flooded with tears. They were not his tears, but the tears of all of Israel who had waited and longed, writing, singing and crying out for God to help His people. They were tears of old that begged once again to have direct contact with God. Here before him was the answer to the many supplications of Israel; here before him was a messenger of God among them once again.

"Oh Yosef, look! He smiles at you," Mary said.

Finally, Joseph looked at the Babe, and to his astonishment he saw the face of Mary.

He smiled. *Of course He would look like His mother: who else was He to look like? God? No one could see the Face of God and live. This Child was destined to be seen by many. He was to be of human estate, and therefore, being human, had to look like His human mother. He was Mary's Child.*

"You must take the Child and put Him upon your knee, to show proper legitimacy and acceptance."

Joseph sprung to his feet. He wanted to object, but he had lost his power to disagree. He knew she was right, and he had to do what was to be.

The radiance of the light still poured from the Babe, and intimidated Joseph.

Mary rose and extended the Babe to him.

With tense arms and unsure legs, he held out his arms to accept the Babe, but felt unable to take hold of Him. Mary seemingly understood, and softly placed the Infant in his embrace. Joseph quickly sat on a pile of hay and placed the Babe on his lap, then with humility he slowly brought the Child to him and cradled Him in his arms. The Babe looked at Joseph and smiled, then moved His eyes around the stable, capturing with curiosity all that was around Him.

Joseph recited the prayer fathers said on the birth of a son, giving thanks to God. In a soft humble voice, Joseph said:

"HaTov VeHameitiv…

Blessed are You, Lord our God, King of the Universe."

When he finished the prayer, he fell into silence. Finally in a trembling voice, he said, "Miryam, I hold a messenger from El Shaddai. I have fear, but I am not afraid. What manner of life are we to have with this Child?"

"I do not know, Yosef, but I trust in El Shaddai. I know Who He is from the angel's declaration and from my cousin Elishevah's revelation. Even the animals acknowledge Who He is. Look at how attentive they are. They look at Him in silence as if they know Him. Even the creatures of the night and all of nature is silent tonight. I hear no nightly noises nor the howl of the wind. This Babe is proof of how much El Shaddai loves us. Yet look at who El Shaddai allowed to be here to welcome Him? Animals, nature and us. That is all that is wanted or needed. We have been told of this happening and accepted it. Our first duty is to know Him, to be of service to Him, and above all to love Him."

From history and from his childhood when he was asked the fourth question at Seder, Joseph heard the question from Passover:

"Ma nishtanah halailah hazeh mikol haleilot?

Why is this night different from any other night?"

The question from long ago belonged to this night. As God had protected His people so many years ago, so this night He was again passing over them and offering them His protection.

Mary slowly returned to the hay on the floor of the cave and rested on her sleeping mat.

"Yosef, I am tired. If it is acceptable to you, I would like to rest."

"Rest, Miryam." Joseph said, feeling the comfort of the Baby in his arms.

Joseph was surprised by His alertness. He squirmed and wiggled in the tight bounds of the swaddling clothes. Every time He looked at Joseph, He smiled. Suddenly the Babe began to whimper and Joseph became alarmed.

"Are you cold?" he asked. He reached for another blanket, and wrapped it around the Child quickly. "Please, please, don't cry. I would not know what to do. I know what to do with my other children, but not One as You."

The Babe smiled again, and stared into Joseph's face. *I think He understood what I said*, he thought.

Slowly Joseph began to sway from right to left to right. The Child settled into the monotony of the sway and closed His eyes and freely slipped into sleep. Joseph began to chant:

"Sh'ma Yis'ra'eil Adonai Eloheinu Adonai echad.
Barukh sheim k'vod malkhuto l'olam va'ed.
V'ahav'ta eit Adonai Elohekha b'khol l'vav'kha
uv'khol naf'sh'kha uv'khol m'odekha.

Hear, Israel, the Lord is our God, the Lord is One.

Blessed be the Name of His glorious kingdom for

ever and ever!

And you shall love the Lord your God with all your

heart and with all your soul and with all your might."

When he finished the prayer, the Babe smiled in His slumber. Joseph felt at ease. The tension in his body slowly ebbed and his courage returned. He felt like a father.

What have I ever done to make this happen to me? How can this be? What good have I done to be so blessed? Help my confusion go away, I ask. Please, help me to be a father to this Being You have sent to Your Chosen People. May He become a great Teacher according to Your will.

The Babe cuddled closer in the crease of Joseph's arm. He had stopped swaying for fear that too much would wake the sleeping Child. He looked around the stable and again felt a quick twinge of failure.

He spoke to the Child in his heart. *You are dealing with a very simple man—a simple man with simple needs and accomplishments. I am a fixer of broken things and a woodworker. I am a father stumbling through parenthood with little instruction, destined to make many mistakes. I will do stupid things. I will fail. Please, be patient with me, and please tell me what I am to do. No child comes with directions, and no parents truly know what they are doing. You are far different from my other children. I do not know what advice I am to give You. I do not know what I should do to help You achieve what You have been sent to do. I do not know where You are to go or what You are to do. Am I supposed to give direction? Advise You? Is it possible there are things You do not know? Is it expected that I tell You, or show You? Is it possible that one like me is expected to tell one so great as You how to be?*

He was fearful, but then he smiled, for he had feared when his other children were born. He imagined every man was fearful, for fathering was a great vocation— one that held many hours of uncertainty and insecurity and many hours of doubts and alarm for his child. He was certain that even God, in spite of knowing all things, had worried about Adam. A child is given what he needs, and then uses it in his own way, not that of his father.

Does El Shaddai see things in me that I do not see? Am I to be a part of what You are here to do? What did El Shaddai see in me that made Him think I was the one who would lead You on Your journey? What does He think I can give You or do for You? Where am I to take You on this earth? I do not know if it is for me to correct You when You do something wrong; how can I? Oh please, help me to know what I am to do, how I am to act. When I am without knowledge, and I ask El Shaddai for help, please ask Him to answer me quickly so that I can be a part of what is to be.

Joseph felt his arms grow tense and he was fearful again. The Babe squirmed, forcing Himself deeper into the curve of Joseph's muscular arms to become more comfortable.

Someday soon, You must help me to know all the things that You know. You will soon find out that I know only what the Rabbis and Elders have told me, and what I feel. My life…my experiences are limited. You will become a wiser Man than I and a far better Person than I am. Someday You must tell me why I was chosen to do so great and so important a thing as to guard a messenger from El Shaddai.

He stopped, for suddenly he felt foolish and ridiculous for repeating himself.

"Forgive me for being so bold and foolish, but I am curious," he said aloud.

Joseph glanced over to where Mary was lying on her mat. She slept soundly. He realized how tired she must have been. The Baby in his arm was also sleeping soundly; His day must have been even more tiring, for He came from a place far different from where He was now. Joseph walked softly across the cave and gently placed the Babe in the manger next to his mother. He covered them both with the largest blanket they had. He felt contented, for he had provided all he could for Mary and the Child. He saw Mary's hand instinctively reach for the Child and protectively rest her hand on Him. Joseph realized that there will always be a bond stronger than any other between son and mother. This one was to be a bond greater than any known in the world. Suddenly, he felt he was not a part of this bond. It was not meant to be. He knew this with certainty.

Suddenly, outside the cave, he heard mumbling, shuffling of feet, and the small slipping and tumbling of stones on the path to the stable. He reached for his heavy wooden staff and gripped it sternly.

What new challenge is this? he thought.

From out of the cold night shadows, images appeared. They were shepherds. Shepherds were at the very bottom of the social ladder among the Jews. They were as low as tax collectors and dung sweepers. There were two of them, with a young shepherd boy. Joseph's mind flashed to King David and he wondered why he thought this. His instinct was to chase them away, but as he looked at their dark, dirty and unkempt faces, he mellowed.

Joseph went out to meet them. In the moonlight, he could see their curiosity and many questions and doubts on their faces; in this he found kinship with them. With great excitement, they spoke to Joseph of what had happened to them. The skies had opened up and a multitude of angels had sung—beautifully sung—songs that still echoed in their ears. They had been told to seek the Child. Joseph smiled, remembering the sounds of singing that he had heard earlier that night. The shepherds spoke excitedly and asked to see the Child, but Joseph quickly rebuked them. Mary had just had a child. In the Law of Moses, she had entered *Nivvah*—the period of blood issuing after childbearing—and was therefore unclean.

"Yosef, what is it?" Mary asked.

He left the shepherds and went inside the cave. He knew they were craning their necks to see the Babe. He told Mary what they had told him and even mentioned the singing he had heard earlier.

"Let them come and see," Mary said.

"But Miryam, you are not purified…"

"They are the children of Israel. He came for them. He is not ours alone. He belongs to all."

She stopped, not wanting him to know that she had no issue of blood and therefore there was no need for *Nivvah*. Her silence allowed Joseph to absorb the wisdom in her words. "Truly it is the will of El Shaddai," Mary added softly.

Joseph agreed, and told the shepherds to enter. As they slowly stepped inside, they froze in wonder at the sight. They stood in silence for a long time, then one by one they knelt down. They prayed in low hesitating mumbles, hiding their newfound spiritual excitement, and not wanting to wake the Babe. They asked if there was anything they could do for the family. Mary and Joseph thanked them. One shepherd removed his cloak and gave it to cover the Babe; Mary and Joseph returned it with a "thank you."

Mary said gently, "You can pray and give praise to El Shaddai for what you know and see." Slowly they began to praise God in voices that grew in volume.

The shepherd boy softly played a flute and Mary smiled at him. She recognized the melody and began to sing a lullaby to the Babe. The night filled with peace and warmth and goodness. The disappointment of failure, the chill of poverty, the aloneness of rejection all dissolved and the cave, the stable became a soft place.

The boy gave the Child a lamb, which Mary and Joseph graciously accepted. Then the shepherds went out and began telling everyone they met of the wonders of the night.

In the early morning, the innkeeper and his wife came to see if they were well. They stayed with Mary while Joseph went to register. While registering, he met his brother Cleopas who told Joseph there soon would be room for them at the inn where he was staying.

"It is humble lodging yet better than what you now have. Come and find comfort," his brother said.

The next day Cleopas, his wife Mary, and their oldest son James, arrived to help Joseph and Mary move to the inn. For three days and nights the families stayed together. Then Mary and Joseph moved to the house of one of their relatives in Bethlehem. They had to stay for the next forty days because Mary according to the Mosaic Law was "unclean." "And the Lord spoke to Moses, saying: 'Speak to the children of Israel, and thou shalt say to them; if a woman having received seed shall bear a man child, she shall be unclean seven days, according to the days of the separation of her flowers, and on the eighth day the infant shall be circumcised: but she shall remain thirty-three days in the blood of her purification. She shall touch no holy thing neither shall she enter into the sanctuary until the days of her purification be fulfilled.'"

Seven days after the birth of the Babe a *mohel* arrived and the Child was circumcised and given the name, *Yeshua*—Jesus, which meant: The Lord is salvation.

When the next thirty-three days were completed, Mary and Joseph took Jesus up to Jerusalem, which was five miles to the north: about a three-hour journey. This trip had a twofold purpose: the purification of Mary and the fulfillment of the third ordinance the Law commanded regarding the firstborn son. This Ordinance was decreed by God to Moses, and dated back to the time of the Exodus. "And the Lord spoke to Moses, saying: 'Sanctify unto Me every firstborn that openeth the womb among the children of Israel as well of men as of beast; for they are all Mine.'" The Teachers of the *Torah* believed that this ordinance was a reckoning for the "passing over" by the Angel of Death of all Israelite children in the great plague that had killed the firstborn of man and beast in Egypt. The first born of Israel had been spared, so they had forfeited their lives and they belonged to God. All children born to the Jews had to be ransomed or redeemed: "bought back" by their parents. The life of the first born was redeemed by a life of innocence—a spotless lamb. Through the death of an innocent substitute, man could be restored to God's grace and show his bond and fellowship with God. So it was set in the law that a life would be paid for a life.

Mary and Joseph's poverty released them from the obligation of sacrificing a lamb. Two turtledoves or two young pigeons: one for a burnt offering and the other for a sin offering, would be given. The Temple priest would offer the two as atonement.

When Mary and Joseph arrived in Jerusalem, they entered through the Fountain Gate. As they walked the winding streets of the city, they ignored all the busyness and went directly to the Temple and through the *Shuldah* Gate. This led into the huge Court of the Gentiles. This Court had been designated as a "house of prayer for all nations" to follow the words of God through Isaiah. But over time, it had been converted into cattle stalls, filled with their odor and noise. Guides waited to provide tours of the premises, and Temple priests wearing white robes and tubular hats directed pilgrims and advised them on what kind of sacrifices were to be performed.

Joseph and Mary passed a rocky wall that contained the warning in Greek and Latin to all Gentiles that they should go no further. On the south wall of the Temple, the Royal Stoa, they purchased from the Temple vendors two turtledoves. Passing through the Gate Beautiful, they entered the Court of the Women. Mary then climbed fifteen semicircular steps that led to the beautiful bronze Nicanor Gate. She could go no further for beyond this Gate was the area reserved for only *koheniym*—priests—and other Jewish men. From this point she could see the Court of Israelites, the Court of Priests, and some of the interior of the holy place of the Temple. A Temple priest came out to greet her. The offering was given to the priest who then walked further into the Temple to make the sacrifice. A group of men and women who were called "The Quiet in the Land" had placed themselves in the Temple to pray daily for the *Messiah* to come. Many of them waited not for a *Messiah* of glory or earthly might, but one of righteousness and spirituality. Many of these people prayed for the honor and blessing to be able to see the *Messiah* before they died. Those keeping this vigil had been preceded by many others. They were a fixture in the Temple, accepted by many as pious and sincere people, and thought by others to be fools.

On that warm Judean day, several faithful "Quiet in the Land" were present when Mary and Joseph took the Child to the Temple. Among them was a man named Simeon, who was "a righteous and devout" man waiting "for the consolation of Israel." He had prayed that he not die before seeing the Messiah. In a dream he had received a promise that his prayers had been heard and he would see the Messiah before he closed his eyes in death. Daily he arrived at the Temple to wait. He loyally continued to pray. Years passed, and now as an old man, his body began to offer him problems. He was having difficulty walking without assistance. He ached and pained with each step. His back was constantly troubling him. His hair had grown shallow and white. Lately his stomach was in turmoil with a dull continual pain, and on the day of the Family's arrival, his head ached. He knew the Messiah was near, for God was making it known to Simeon that his name was soon to be called.

He stood with the others in prayer, each bobbling and bowing in reverent rhythm to their spoken prayers. Suddenly Simeon grew weak, and with disappointment he sat and mentally begged forgiveness of God for his weakness. He closed his eyes and hoped the edge of pain would dissipate. He was secluded from all that surrounded him. Several peaceful and silent moments passed. Then he heard a small whimper, a small sigh. At first he ignored it, but the sign lingered, and suddenly it awakened within him a new and different reality.

He knew and recognized it as the breath of life! The breath of a new life!

He opened his eyes and saw a small woman attentively carrying a Child in her arms; she was followed by a sturdy young man. Their faces were shadowed behind veil and hood and when he did see their faces they were engraved with solemnity. Simeon was compelled to stand. His heart beat vigorously. His body moistened with perspiration. His mouth grew dry. The shadow of the couple passed over him and all the pains and discomforts of the years were stilled. A bright blinding light bloomed inside him and his many years of prayer became one prayer.

"Na'arah—Young girl," he said softly. Mary, with the restless Baby in her arms, stopped and turned to him. Quickly and without thought he said, "Almah—maiden, may I?" He extended his arms. Mary looked quickly to Joseph and finding approval, carefully gave the Child to Simeon.

As soon as the weight of the Baby came to his arms, his eyes filled with tears and he slowly raised the Baby Jesus above his head so that he had to look up into the heavens. In a loud voice, he blessed and praised God. Then he slowly lowered the Baby and cradled Him in his arms. He spoke—to no one present yet to everyone—"Now Thou dost dismiss Thy servant, O Lord, according to Thy Word in peace because my eyes have seen Thy salvation, Which Thou hast prepared before the face of all peoples: a light to the revelation of the Gentiles and the glory of Thy people Israel."

Mary and Joseph looked at each other in surprise for they both wondered how this old man knew about Jesus. They politely smiled an acknowledgement.

For an instant longer, the old man held the Child Jesus, Who now was content in his arms. With great humility, Simeon blessed Joseph and Mary and thanked them for allowing him the honor of holding the Babe. As he was about to return Jesus to Mary, his heart grew heavy and the weight of time to come pressed against him. He foresaw a demanding task ahead for the couple and many things passed through his mind. He grew sad, and yet happy that he would not witness what he saw. The Baby grew heavier in his arms. He knew that this heaviness was not for the Baby but for the young mother, so he looked long and hard into her young face, looking for signs of courage, signs of acceptance.

Mary looked at Simeon with a question in her eyes, and then as if she had unrolled a scroll, she opened to him and he saw her inner being. Her eyes now displayed the courage and acceptance for which Simeon searched.

He placed the Baby in her open arms. Her arms did not bend under the weight of the Baby, as Simeon's had. With tears of joy in his eyes and yet great sorrow in his voice he said, "Behold this Child is set for the fall, and for the resurrection of many in Israel, and for a sign which shall be contradicted." Looking directly into Mary's eyes, he said in an even more mournful voice: "And thy own soul a sword shall pierce, that out of many hearts thoughts may be revealed."

Mary did not flinch under the pressure of the prophesy, but looked at the old man with great love.

Simeon fell back and was assisted by those near him. His eyes slipped from Mary's face to Joseph. He saw even greater pain in his future, but Simeon closed his eyes and begged God to have him see no more, to know no more. He sat surrounded by many who asked him questions, but his mind was on the young parents and on God, for He had kept His promise to Simeon and to Israel and to the world.

Joseph took Mary's arm and gently led her away. He looked back at Simeon with displeasure. He guided Mary through the gate and into the Court of Women. As they passed through the gate, the daughter of Phanuel of the tribe of Aser, a prophetess named Hannah, who for years, like Simeon, had prayed and fasted day and night at the Temple approached. She had heard what Simeon had said. As Joseph and Mary passed her, she loudly praised God and proclaimed to all that the redemption of Israel was at hand.

Seeing that many were gathering, Joseph quickly moved away, sheltering Mary and Jesus with his body. They passed quickly through the crowds and soon were out of the city and back on the road back to Bethlehem. As they journeyed on, Joseph walked with a heavy heart, for what the old man had said to Mary disturbed him greatly. The old man's face was etched in his mind's eye and the words the man spoke burned in his ears. His heart was heavy with concern and sadness.

How can Mary, this young servant of El Shaddai, who has risked life and family to do His will, be rewarded with sorrow and pain in her life? Had El Shaddai forgotten His promise to protect and guard Jesus and Mary?

"Ishi—husband, you are troubled."

Mary's statement took him from the Temple and the Old Man to the real moment around him.

"That man. The old one at the Temple who predicted that you would suffer many sorrows, has disturbed me greatly."

He looked back at Mary and found her face flushed with tears and her eyes red from crying. He left the reins of the mule to emptiness and rushed back to her.

"Be not concerned, Ishi. I cry not for myself, nor the sorrow that the prophet spoke of, but I cry for our Son who will not be accepted. I now see He will be like so many great prophets of El Shaddai who were treated cruelly by our people."

"Still I am concerned, and I ache for what seems so unfair. Please stop crying for this brings me more sadness."

"Let me cry now, for when these sorrows come to me, I must be strong and stand as a witness to my faith in El Shaddai."

Joseph silently acknowledged learning another lesson from Mary. She was far stronger in faith than he. He stood silently by her side knowing that this was all he could do; this was all he had to do.

Then he thought of her words—*a prophet! Mary had spoken of a prophet. Jesus will be a prophet, not a rabbi.*

He became overjoyed. He felt he could cry with joy.

Of course the Almighty has remained silent for almost four hundred years, and He wishes to show the Israelites that He has not forsaken or forgotten them. He wishes to remind us of His loving authority. He again wishes to bring us back to Him. The Almighty has blessed His Chosen People with a new prophet.

Sometime later as they neared Bethlehem, Joseph began to admonish himself. *Why must I always be so rash? Why do I always place myself before El Shaddai? Why can I not be as sure as Miryam is?*

He glanced behind him at Mary as she sat on the mule and shielded Jesus with her body and veil. Her protection of Jesus warmed Joseph, and he knew he had to become as protective of the Child and unbending to the things of the world as she was. He basked in the idea that he too was to be the protector of a prophet. He recognized that he was to be part of a great new beginning for the Chosen People. A new prophet was among them and he was part of the plan: to give this prophet a place to live and sleep. He had to prepare this Child in the ways of Judaism; it was his fatherly duty. Quickly he vowed to study the *Torah* more diligently.

His thoughts returned to the Temple and the Old Man. He still saw him holding Jesus and heard his voice, and once again a chill ran through his body.

For him to say that, for him to see into the future and predict that Miryam would suffer much, he must have had an angel like Miryam and me and the shepherds. How many angels has El Shaddai dispatched to earth for this prophet?

He paused.

No! I doubt the old man had an angel. He was perhaps just wise and knew the history of our people. I resented and opposed him; likewise, I am sure he knew that no prophet has ever been welcomed by his people. Israel has never readily accepted the Word or Words of God.

Once again he became bothered; most prophets had a hard and difficult life. He did not want this for his young charge. How could he make things better for Jesus?

There you go again, Yosef, wanting to change the will and ways of El Shaddai…will you ever learn? Will you ever be as peaceful and resigned as Miryam? When will you learn that if something comes from El Shaddai, no matter how displeasing it may be, it should be received with respect and obedience?

He begged God to forgive him but added to his prayer: *But please give me understanding, for I walk more blindly now than before and I need Your guidance.*

*

Joseph and Mary decided not to tell anyone in the family about what had happened in the Temple. Mary did not want the prophecy to darken the joy in her heart at the birth of Jesus. It was too great and important a moment for her and for the Jewish nation. Joseph wanted to make the life of Jesus simple, without prying eyes and questions. He was certain that all was in God's plan and the plan would keep him and his family safe. He was also certain that because Mary had been so great a servant of God that nothing of great pain would befall her.

The next day Joseph and his brother Cleopas began maintenance repairs on the two carts that had carried the women and children. The poor roads had taken a heavy toll on the axles and wheels. The caravan back to Nazareth would depart in two days so they needed to hurry with their repairs.

The house of Joseph's distant cousin where Joseph and Mary had finally found refuge was located at the very end of the village. In fact, it was the last house passed when leaving Bethlehem. The crude dirty road leaving Bethlehem to the east led to the limestone ridge of the Judean highlands.

In spite of its historical and religious background few people visited the little village. Caravans usually did not stop, and if they did, the village people found their entertainment in sitting on their rooftops or nearby hills to watch.

Joseph worked hard to secure the wheels of the cart and when he finished, he decided to begin making a small cradle for Jesus. As he shaved the wood to a smooth surface an unexpected strong breeze from the east passed him. The shavings and dust from his work scattered all around him, and he covered his eyes with the back of his hand. He glanced up at one of the nearby hills and saw a large caravan passing along the ridge. Their silhouettes were outlined against the late day sun.

He smiled. *Another caravan that passes by little Bethlehem*, he thought as he returned to his work. Moments later his concentration was disturbed by the joyful and excited sounds of the village children. He stopped working and stood erect. To his surprise he witnessed the caravan slowly sauntering through the narrow streets of Bethlehem. Children noisily ran beside the caravan with glee and amazement.

About twenty or twenty-five camels walked slowly and tediously through the village. Men and women dressed in a rainbow of colors walked silently beside each camel. Several men were armed with swords, knives and lances. Other men rode the camels in a variety of saddles. Several camels were bedecked with cloth necklaces, chest bands and knee coverings. The remaining animals were loaded down with supplies and other necessities to survive the desert voyage.

Three camels in particular were elaborately decorated with long fringes and tassels hanging down their backs and sides. One rider was shaded by an umbrella with long tassels that swayed to the rhythm of the camel's paces. The other two sat under thinly veiled canopies with many tassels swinging back and forth. Everyone in the caravan was richly dressed in three primary groups of colors. One group was dressed in red and yellow with white turbans and scarves that partially covered their faces. Another group was robed in blue and white with black turbans and scarves across their faces. The last group was donned in purple and white with beige turbans and scarves. Each group seemed to belong to one of the richly dressed riders under the umbrella and canopies. Joseph estimated a total of forty-five people.

The long caravan passed directly by the shop and house where Joseph worked. They continued on until they came to a large clearing just outside of the village and near Joseph's shop. The moment the camels and travelers stopped, a frenzy of activity followed. Camels barked and people shouted, while others ran around doing many things that seemed important only to them. One thing was certain: they were in a great hurry to unload the camels, build their tents, start fires and get settled.

Joseph stood watching in astonishment. He had never seen a caravan this elaborate up close, nor such frantic activity. The camels intrigued him the most. He wondered what it would be like to ride such an animal. His brother Cleopas, who had ridden one once, told Joseph that it made him feel powerful, for he was high above the earth and everyone and everything. Cleopas said that the steps of the camel and the sway of its walk made him feel like a baby being rocked in his mother's arms. Joseph tried to imagine, but it seemed useless so he shook his head. Certainly Cleopas was just being creative. He returned to shaving the wood for the cradle, for it had to be finished. Soon, he forgot all about the bustle of humanity in the distance.

Near sunset, Joseph stood erect to soothe the ache in his back. He had worked hard all day and his clothing was drenched with perspiration. He needed water. He moved to the nearby table to get his cup. Suddenly the air around him was filled with the scent of frankincense. He turned quickly and saw three men splendidly dressed in the finest materials he had ever seen standing outside his workshop. Each man was bejeweled with rings, arm bands and necklaces. Joseph stared at the grandeur before him.

The men were of different sizes. The short, pudgy one was clothed in red and gold with a flat dish-like headpiece. His face was round, his eyes slightly slanted, and though Joseph was not sure, he believed that the man's skin was yellow. The medium-sized man was dressed in blue and white with a pointed headpiece; his face was long with an equally long white beard. He looked a great deal like many men in Bethlehem. The last man was tall, thin, and dressed in purple and white with a white turban on his head. The white material contrasted against his black skin.

A few awkward silent moments passed between the strangers and Joseph.

"Miryam," Joseph called, his voice tinged with caution and wonder. He did not take his eyes from the three men.

From the house, he heard Mary's soft voice reply, "One moment, Yosef."

The black stranger said, "Good day, good sir. My name is Balthazar." Pointing to the other richly dressed men, he continued, "This is Kasper, and this is Melchior: my companion Magi. We seek a king."

"We have followed a star by day and night and it came to rest here above your house," the short one called Kasper said, waving his hand above his head. "Is there a king here?"

"We were informed by King Herod that the King of the Jews was to be born in Bethlehem. We have followed the star for many, many miles and it rests above us now," Melchior said.

Joseph wanted to walk out into the late afternoon light to see if the star truly was above them, but he smothered the thought when he heard the sounds of Mary's shuffling feet. They grew louder then stopped. He sensed she stood directly behind him. He could hear small infant sounds from Jesus.

"I am sorry, sirs, but there is no king here. I live here with my wife, Miryam, and our Son Yeshua and my other children." Joseph stepped aside to reveal Mary and Jesus. He looked proudly at his family. When he returned his attention to the men he was shocked to see them on their knees, bowing low to the ground. They finally stood and began to speak in languages that Joseph and Mary did not understand.

Mary leaned close to Joseph and whispered, "They were praying to Yeshua and adoring Him as King of the Jews."

Joseph wondered briefly about Mary's knowledge of the foreigners' words. "Sirs, we are simple people," he said aloud. The Magi began to talk excitedly to each other and finally, after a short debate, turned to Joseph and Mary.

"We understand your concern," Balthazar said, looking around at the small crowd that had gathered. "We have traveled far and we may be mistaken. Please accept our apology and our intrusion."

The three men backed away and returned quickly to one of the large tents.

Joseph guided Mary back into the house, looking over his shoulder at the tents. "I am so glad we leave soon," Mary said. "We do not want to draw too much attention. I fear what that would lead to."

Joseph nodded his head in agreement, but his mind remained on the stranger's big tent.

Later, he returned to the back of the house and stood watching the biggest tent. It looked so permanent—like a citadel not of might but of determination. He remembered the words of Balthazar: "...we seek a king." Suddenly Joseph's knees weakened. His thoughts went to Mary who had understood the languages of the three strangers. Then again he heard "...we have followed a star..." and: "the King of the Jews..." This time his knees gave way and he reached for a stool to sit upon.

The idea raced wildly through his mind, and the thought of the greatness of "the King of the Jews" exploded. Images of palaces, thrones, robes, and grandeur like that of the three strangers flashed before him.

El Shaddai has given His Chosen People a King! Joseph thought. The enormity of this stuck in his mind until he suddenly realized, *I am to serve the "King of the Jews"!* He became overwhelmed and then crushed, and finally frightened. His heart raced and he experienced difficulty breathing. In the grips of fear, he searched for help.

Do not be so sure of what you heard, or what you think, Yosef, he told himself. *You are being a fool. These men of the stars are not even Jews. Why would they be looking for the 'King of the Jews'? What do they know of the Jews? Why would El Shaddai entrust the King of His people to you? A young maiden of strong faith, a poor beginning, a stable birth, ignorant, unworthy shepherds to greet Him, and wondering, lost, and confused Magi.*

What kind of beginning is that for a king? Especially a King begotten of El Shaddai? No, Yosef, this time you have concluded incorrectly, for such beginnings are for a lowly rabbi and a plain prophet but not a royal King. He felt his body return to normal and he stopped perspiring.

It is all a mistake. Even the three strangers admitted they were mistaken and apologized. He sat silently on the stool for a few more moments, and then turned his attention to closing up the wood shop and joining his family for the evening meal.

Sometime later, long after life had slowed down and night had settled, the three men appeared again at the house of Joseph and Mary. They stood in silence and waited. Joseph and Mary had no idea how long they had been standing by the house, but when they found them, Joseph invited them inside the house quickly. When they were granted entry, they again fell down in adoration at the feet of Mary who held Jesus. The Child sat regally and fully alert on His mother's lap. His serious face beamed with understanding and glowed with acceptance.

Joseph wondered: *Could it be that Yeshua understands what these men are about?*

The man called Kasper removed from one of the folds of his clothing a small wooden box, and laid it at Mary's feet.

"We know that the King will reveal Himself in His time, but be assured His secret will remain with us and us alone. I give Him a small chest of gold to satisfy His Kingship."

The one called Melchior then produced a small chest from the folds of his apparel and laid it at the feet of Mary.

"We understand your fears but they cannot compare to the fears we have had if we had mistaken this Child. I give Him a small chest of frankincense to remind Him of the Temple; may the smoke become prayers before His God."

Balthazar produced a yellow cloth of the finest silk and slowly unraveled it, then placed a small jar before them.

"We know you are living in uncertainty, but we are certain that He is truly the King of the Jews: a Child that shall grow to help His people and many others. I give Him the gift of myrrh to fill the space around Him with sweetness and may it perfume His way through life and at His death."

The Magi stood, bowed respectfully to Jesus, again to Joseph and Mary, and slowly backed away and disappeared into the shadows of the starry night.

Mary rose from her stool and said simply, "Yosef, please take the gifts given to Jesus and put them away. El Shaddai has once again revealed His will. What has happened here is not of our understanding, but will someday hold great meaning. Yeshua is past His bedtime. I bid you a good night. Shalom."

Joseph remained in his place in complete turmoil. The visitors had caused confusion, but Mary's calm dismissal of what had happened made it worse.

Yeshua is not to be a rabbi, or a prophet, He is to be the King of the Jews! He was sent by El Shaddai to become the new King of the Chosen People. Not since Zedekiah have the Chosen People had a king, and now El Shaddai has chosen a King for His people and a King of His own choosing. A King from obscurity like David of old; a ruler over all His creation like Adam of old.

Suddenly, he thought of Jesse, the father of David, and understood the crushing realization that he must have had when his son was to be king of the Jews. A multitude of thoughts, feelings and emotions surged, raced and sprinted through his mind. He became overwhelmed. His palms moistened and his head pounded and his heart raced. He shuddered and shook his head repeatedly, physically swaying under the fear of his thoughts. Slowly and carefully, with great control, he thought: *To be the father of a rabbi was a privilege; to be the father of a prophet was an honor, but to be the pretended father of a king is humbling.*

He felt like he was going to be ill. He took a shallow breath and slowly allowed the air of pride and acknowledgment slip from his trembling body. His thoughts were quivering with anticipation and a thousand ideas throbbed in his mind.

Finally when he was able to stand without support, he forced himself to think more clearly, but all his thoughts culminated in one idea: *Yeshua was born in the Village of David who was both king and prophet perhaps that is it—Yeshua will be all three—a Rabbi, Prophet and King! Oh, El Shaddai, what have You given me to do? How am I to attend to Him?*

Joseph was on the verge of tears.

Had I known, I would have asked Your forgiveness, El Shaddai, and asked You to find a man more worthy, better equipped for such an undertaking. How could You think that I—Yosef bar Yakov—a carpenter of little means, a man of lesser mentality, could be of any value to You? How can I serve so great a Being as Yeshua?

"Oh how I wish my angel would come and talk to me again," he said aloud.

He closed his eyes, hoping and praying that his wish would be granted.

He was a carpenter who used his hands to live, a Jew who was to obey, a father with great humanity, a man prone to error, who knew small things and never thought or knew of grand things. He was a man who knew how to pray, how to walk in God's world, how to talk to God's people, marvel daily at God's creations, and little else.

How am I to become something different? What changes must I make to become what El Shaddai wants?

Suddenly, images of castles, thrones, armies, guards and slaves passed through Joseph's mind again, and he became frightened by the future. He acknowledged that he would never fit into such a world, but perhaps this was God's plan: he was to be a pillar for Jesus to lean against and nothing more. Perhaps that was why he, Joseph, often found himself asking what he was to be in this family. God wanted him to be the being he was and nothing more.

So Yeshua is to be King, Prophet and Rabbi to our people.

He rapidly moved his hand before his face as if to erase all thoughts and images. He was done with this night. He gathered the gifts, turned quickly and entered the house. He moved quietly to his sleeping mat, said his prayers and rested.

After a few moments, he said aloud, "A King, a Prophet, a Rabbi not wanted by the people."

That night in his sleep Joseph dreamed he was walking through a fierce sand storm. He had never experienced such a storm. The wind ruthlessly pushed sand across a well-constructed road: a road he recognized as one of the Romans' better roads. He was certain it had been constructed for the rapid deployment of Roman infantry and cavalry. The Romans called these roads *Viae Militariae*—the military ways.

The wind blew every grain of sand from the nearby desert yet no sand rested on the road. The howling wind began to resemble the wails of human beings in pain. The grains of sand stung and bit at his uncovered flesh. The wind tugged and swept his beard and clothing to the side of his body. He lowered his head and covered his mouth and nose with part of his hood so he could breathe. Suddenly the wind shifted and he felt it behind him, pushing and shoving him forward. He had no control over his steps. He felt hopelessly lost, helplessly out of control. He had no idea why he traveled this Roman road. He looked up, and in the distance he saw a man moving toward him. Unbelievably, the man was not walking, yet he was drifting toward Joseph. The wind was not bothering this stranger; he seemed outside the sandstorm. The man continued his peaceful approach, with his white cloak draped neatly over his body. The folds of his clothing were perfectly in place; his feet and sandals were hidden under the length of his robe. The man's face was lost in the dark shadows of his hood.

"Yosef!" Suddenly the howl of the wind died. "YOSEF!"

The voice! It was familiar. Joseph's mind raced quickly through time, and suddenly he remembered.

He quickened his steps, and soon Joseph and the stranger faced each other.

"Yes, Yosef. It is I, Malach. You must go back and in haste. Heed my words: Arise, and take the Child and His mother, and fly into the land of Egypt: and be there until I call thee. For it will come to pass that Herod will seek the Child to destroy Him."

The urgency of Malach's voice scared Joseph awake and he found himself wet with perspiration. Without any hesitation, he rose from his sleeping mat and began making preparations for his family's departure. His movements woke Mary, and he told her of his dream. In equal haste, she prepared for Egypt.

"The gifts?" Joseph asked.

"They were given to us for the voyage. We should be able to find a good caravan to take us to Egypt and sustain us for a while."

Before morning arrived, Joseph went to the back of the house. He was shocked to see the tents dismantled, camp broken, camels packed, and the caravan well on its way. He watched the departure and wondered what their coming and going meant in God's plan.

Was their purpose to let me know about the mission of Jesus? he wondered.

Hours later they joined a caravan on its way to Egypt.

Mary asked, "Do you think those travelers left because they had been warned of the danger they had brought to Jesus?"

"I am sure of it. I have come to believe that all that happens to Yeshua, to us, is from the direct hand of El Shaddai. I believe we have an angel, perhaps many angels watching over us. Miryam, nothing ill shall happen to us from any man, not even kings, and we will be out of the reach of all, even the evil one."

"We are guided and guarded by El Shaddai," she agreed. "He seems to perform small miracles for us and to us." As she turned away, she continued, "Like when we understood the language of those strange men."

Joseph jumped as if lightning had struck him. Mary's words and their truth echoed in his mind. He had been part of a miracle and had not known it.

How many other miracles have I experienced without realizing them?

He promised himself to be more alert to the exciting miracles that happen around him. He smiled. He was a part of the mission of Jesus.

Their caravan traveled across Judea and into Gaza. After they rested, they continued southeast to the town called in Hebrew *Raphaiah Rafah*. This was the last outpost before entering the vast desert land known by the Hebrews as the *Seneh*—Sinai. They then traveled along the coastline, which was safer and climatically more appealing.

In the city known in Aramaic as *Seyan*, or to the Romans *Pelusium*, they learned of the killing of the innocent. From that day on, in their thoughts and dreams they often heard the wail of the wounded mothers. They gave thanks to God for His protection and praised Him for His care of them. They stayed in this obscure city for several months before moving further into Egypt to a city on the Nile called *Bubastis Tal Basta* which was named after the Egyptian cat deity

Bastet. Here Joseph established himself as a woodcutter. With the few other Hebrews in the city they complied with the Mosaic Law and enjoyed a time of peace and prosperity.

When Jesus reached the age of three His mother Mary sowed *sisit*—fringe—on His coat. This was done in compliance with the Scriptures that demanded: "Make tassels on the four corners of the cloak you wear." At dawn and in the evening, He would join the Jewish men of the village to sit and listen as the Elders recited the words of the *Shema*. Thereby Jesus grew in the faith of His people through the example of Joseph and the other Jewish men. One night, Joseph had another dream.

Again he was on a road. The day was cloudy and there was a chill in the air. The road he trod was far different from any of the roads he had walked before, in life or in dreams. It was a dirt road, soaked from heavy rain, making it nearly impossible to travel. His feet slipped deep in wet mud with every step. He felt the mud slip between his toes and grip his feet, ankles and calves. He struggled to pull his leg free and maintain his balance. Numerous times, he thought he would fall.

Why have I decided to walk such a road? he wondered. *Why is it necessary for me to travel such a road? Where am I supposed to be going?*

The sun broke suddenly through the clouds and instantly dried the road, yet his feet remained deep in the once muddy road. He looked around for assistance but none was there. Far in the distance, he saw a speck that became a dot, then a form, and finally an image. Another traveler was coming toward him. The traveler was walking without any difficulty. He knew it was Malach—his angel! Joseph stopped his struggling and waited. Malach approached, surrounded by a heavy mist, making his image appear nonhuman. "Shalom, Yosef."

Joseph did not answer him. It was not necessary to greet an angel, for a vision of an angel was not a visit but a blessing.

"Arise and take the Child and His mother, and go into the land of Israel. For they are dead that sought the life of the Child"

With that, Joseph's legs were free and Malach was gone.

Joseph arose from his sleeping mat and immediately began to prepare for their journey back to the land of Israel. He did not stop to analyze this message. He only knew he had to obey and do what was commanded. Deep in his heart, he felt great joy for he knew he would be among his people. He would see his brother and his family again and he and Mary would not be strangers in a strange land.

Several days later, after selling their property and finding a caravan going back to Israel, they returned to the Promised Land. As they neared home, Joseph heard Malach's voice say: "Archaelaus now reigns in the room of Herod his father, be warned: retire to the quarters of Galilee and dwell in the place of Nazareth. For He shall be called a Nazarene." So they entered "the village of Nazareth in Galilee."

*

The Hebrews have always made the home the center of their faith. Many of the Hebrew customs have strong family ties. *Pesach*—Passover—and other high holidays, and the weekly observance of *Shabbath*—Sabbath—were carried from the Temple or Synagogues to the home, and there celebrated with the family. The family was bound by maxims, legends, and traditions interwoven in Judaic life and intertwined in the family.

On the first Friday night in Nazareth, Mary fulfilled her duty as mother and wife of the home by welcoming in the Sabbath. It was a duty of the woman to follow this ancient custom, dating back to Rebecca, one of the matriarchs of Judaism. The wife had the privilege of lighting the Sabbath candles because the mother has more influence over the spirit of the home. After lighting two candles, Mary covered her eyes for a moment, then wound her hands three times around and over the Sabbath candles, reciting the prayer of blessing.

"Barukh atah Adonai Eloheinu, melekh ha'olam, asher kid'shanu b'mitzvotav v'tzivanu l'hadlik ner shel Shabbat.

Blessed are You, Lord our God, King of the universe,

Who has made us holy through His commandments

and commanded us to kindle the Sabbath light."

Then she stood and silently prayed. This ceremony cemented the family unit and made their location a home.

The Judaic faith was a portable religion because it was imbedded in the family, and because Judaism was always being pursued and troubled. The family included the vast extension of relatives. The Hebrew word for family was *aha,* which had its root in the word *ah,* which referred to brother, half/step brother, cousin or any near relative, thus a family included everyone of blood or of commonality.

Joseph and Mary expected to stay permanently in Nazareth. Their time there was happy and peaceful. Mary became a mother to all the children and Joseph provided, guarded and guided. The family accepted its limited economic status with joy. They had what they needed: no more, no less. The secrets Joseph and Mary carried remained secrets, not repeated to anyone or even each other. They grew in faith and were pleased that El Shaddai looked on them with favor. They were Hebrews; they were chosen, and that was all they were happy to be.

Nazareth was a small isolated village in Galilee, covering about fifteen acres. It was agricultural, with three or four hundred citizens in thirty-five to forty houses. It had no great historical landmarks or heroes. It was situated in a bowl on the northern ridge of the Jezreel Valley. It was said that Nazareth was a perfect town to get lost in, for no one visited it, not even stray animals. It was inaccessible except for dirt footpaths, and few had reason to visit. There was only one small well on the northern end of the village, and that was depleting. Nazarenes had to collect rainwater to survive. They built cisterns on the nearby hills to collect whatever rain fell. Despite its insignificance, it was a very scenic place. The rolling hills around the village gave a beautiful view of the Valley. On a clear day, sitting on one of these hills, one could see caravans traveling on their way to Capernaum and other towns and cities. The caravan route would eventually turn to the coast to a Roman road called *Via Maris*—the Way of the Sea.

Now in Nazareth and being good believing Hebrews, Joseph and Mary followed every law set down in their Holy Scriptures. They did not feel that they were special, although special things had happened to them; as devout Jews, they accepted the ancestral belief that they were part of the Chosen People of God. Joseph and Mary simply accepted the daily elations and disappointments of life.

Joseph returned to a new, small woodcutter's shop with a lean-to on the northeastern edge of Nazareth. The shop was purposely built to be the last building before leaving the village so that piles of wood could be stored and not be annoying to the other villagers. Most of those traveling from Nazareth were going to Cana and Capernaum. The house that he, Mary and Jesus occupied was about thirty feet away from his shop. The work shop was plain and simple like those of other artisans in the village.

Joseph was constantly kept busy, for a carpenter's shop was always an indispensable part of any village, town, or city. He made wooden beams for house repairs or constructions, and other items needed for the house such as: doors, slats for fencing, lintels for doors. He built pergolas to be set up along the side of a house. The farmers hired Joseph to make stilts or yokes for their ploughs. Ladies commissioned him to make furniture: cabinets, chests, and bins for storage.

During these early years, Jesus was in the care of His mother. Jewish fathers usually didn't have the patience to feed, change, and tend to the many questions of a young child. But at the age of five, Joseph took Jesus to the shop and began to instruct Him in the art of carpentry and wood repairing. Most of those early years were spent in identification of tools and familiarization of their use.

It was the father's duty to begin religious instruction of his child. One of the first things Joseph taught Jesus was the *Asereth ha Dibroth*—the Ten Commandments. When Jesus was ten, Joseph taught Him the traditions of the Hebrew people. Then Jesus was given over to the rabbi and Elders of the Synagogue to prepare Him for His Blessing and Prayers. The rabbi often came to Joseph and Mary to report that Jesus was well advanced in His understanding of the Lord. They found Him to be an exciting student, who asked challenging questions. Joseph beamed with pride.

They watched Him play tag, leap frog, hide and seek. They saw him collect stones and twigs and refine and smooth them. Sometimes the children made sand houses and used the stones and twigs to decorate or reinforce them.

Jesus had a natural ability as a leader among the children. He was more mature than the others and often He gently corrected a wrongdoing or instructed a misguided child.

At the age of twelve, Jesus had His Blessing and Praise and became a "man" and had to bear the religious responsibilities of a Hebrew man. On the Sabbath morn of His becoming a "Son of the Law," Joseph, Cleopas, and their other male relatives walked with Him to the synagogue. There Jesus read the *parashah*—the prescribed passage for the day from the *Pentateuch*.

Joseph beamed with great pride as he watched Jesus unroll the scroll. He nostalgically recalled his own becoming a "Son of the Law." When Jesus began to read, Joseph felt a chill shudder through him, for he knew that the passage had special meaning for him. For the first time in his journey of obedience, Joseph felt that God revealed to him all that he had not known. Standing on the *bimah*—podium, Jesus read:

"Ki-yeled Yulad-lanu ben nitr-lanu.

For a CHILD IS BORN TO US, and a Son is given to us, and the government is upon His shoulders; and His name shall be called, Wonderful, Counselor, God the Mighty, the Father of the world to come, the Prince of Peace. His empire shall be multiplied, and there shall be no end of peace: He shall sit upon the throne of David, and upon His kingdom; to establish it and strengthen it with judgment and with justice, from henceforth and forever: the zeal of the Lord of hosts will perform this."

That night after the celebrations had ceased, and Mary and Joseph were alone, she said, "You are exceptionally proud today, Yosef. I know this is an important day, but you personally have found a great significance to this day."

Joseph looked at Mary, and with a wide smile on his lips he replied, "Isha—wife, I now know what Yeshua is to do in this life. I received confirmation today and I now know all."

Mary smiled and uttered a joyous mental thanks to God, for she knew that her husband had been unsettled and bewildered. She knew he had searched for many years to find what his mission in this family created by God.

From that day on, when Jesus went to the synagogue, He wore the *tallith* prayer shawl. Now as a "Son of the Law," he was permitted to conduct the Sabbath service. Now empowered to officiate, He could step up to the *Aron habrit*—the Ark of the Covenant—in the wall facing south toward Jerusalem, pronounce benedictions, sing responsive verses from the Psalms with the congregation, and carry the Sacred Scroll of the Law in solemn procession around the synagogue.

With each passing day, Jesus seemed to mature. Joseph noticed this change, and he silently backed away, knowing that this was God's way of fulfilling what Jesus was to do and be. He knew that his Son was becoming so different—so intense—through God, and not through his own efforts. Jesus was from God and all was in God's hands. In silence he watched as Jesus grew in wisdom. He watched as Jesus explained to anyone the most complicated wording of the Scriptures. His words made everything seem easy to understand. Jesus lived the Holy Scriptures far more easily than any other person of Jewish blood.

When someone was in need, Jesus was first to assist them. When someone was injured, Jesus was there to help and His instruction for healing always seemed to work. The most arrogant, disliked, ill-tempered neighbors in the village were warmly received and made impotent by Jesus's calm gentle voice.

Joseph was pleased by the manner and degree of respect Jesus showed to Mary. He had a way of saying *"Immi"* that carried a depth of meaning and a stronger bond, which Joseph could sense but not fully understand. It reached back to the beginnings of life in Eden and continued into endless time.

Joseph became aware that Jesus was looking at him in a different way. Jesus began to do things that changed their relationship.

He stopped holding Joseph's hand when they traveled or when in a large crowd.

Suddenly He did not ask Joseph about the Holy Writings, or seek his advice on carpentry. He asked fewer questions for He seemed to know all the answers.

He was more knowledgeable than many boys His age.

Joseph sensed that Jesus had a great understanding of him. There were times he was sure Jesus, like Mary, could read his thoughts and know his feelings. Joseph was certain that Jesus knew of the private difficulties that His parents had experienced. Joseph did not feel uncomfortable under Jesus's gaze; he felt assured of His compassion and understanding. Jesus understood Joseph's simple humanity, just as He understood the humanity of all those who came His way.

Soon after Jesus's "Blessing and Prayers," the Hebrews celebrated the high Holy Day of *Pesach* Passover. Joseph and his brother Cleopas, their families and many relatives went to Jerusalem for this feast. While in Jerusalem, they decided to remain and celebrate the holiday of Shavout, the Feast of Weeks. This holiday was fifty days after Passover and had several other names. It had been called *Hag HaKatzir*, the Feast of the Harvest Holiday, and *Yom Bikkurim*, the Holiday of First Fruits. It was a joyous holiday of thanksgiving and the offering of the new grain of the summer harvest to God. It was always celebrated in the Hebrew month of *Sivan* and normally on the sixth, seventh or eighth day of that month. The families wanted to celebrate this holiday and give thanks for all the blessings and benefits they had received. Not being farmers, they would symbolically offer the fruits of their beings—their children—to God.

In preparing for their journey, they decided to travel along the beautiful coastline roads of the Roman *Mare Nostrum*—Our Sea: The Mediterranean. These roads, called the *Via Maris* by the Romans, were constantly being repaired and patrolled by the Roman army. They would pass by Mount Carmel, and proceed to the port city of Caesarea, also called *Caesarea Palaestinae* or *Caesarea Maritima* by the Romans and *Qesari* by the Jews. The city was built by Herod the Great and named after the Emperor Caesar Augustus. This city was famous for its artificial harbor, and was the naval base for the Herodian navy which aided the Romans in the Mediterranean and journeyed to the far off *Pontus Euxinos*—Black Sea. Their route would take them over the *HaSharon*—Plain of Sharon—until they came to the port city of Joppa. From this seaport they would turn east to Lydda, pass the town of Arimathaea, go through Emmaus, and finally reach Jerusalem.

Their extended families gave the appearance of a long caravan, and everyone enjoyed the togetherness of family. They sang, laughed, and told stories of their family's bygone members and histories.

When they arrived, they found lodging with distant relatives, friends and business associates, and with gratitude and humility accepted whatever housing they were offered. They spent several days in Jerusalem in a state of spiritual euphoria. Together they went to the Temple, and prayed prayers of thanksgiving for the goodness of God, and when all the festivities passed, they prepared for their journey back to Nazareth.

Mary, her sister Salome and her sister's husband Zebedee decided to leave earlier to visit with some elderly relatives who lived in Emmaus, a day's journey from Jerusalem. After the visit, Mary and the others would wait for Joseph and his family to arrive. Joseph and Cleopas and his family decided to stay in the Holy City a day more and socialize with some business associates.

Mary presumed that Jesus would remain in Jerusalem with Joseph; Joseph presumed Jesus was with Mary because of the strong attachment He had to His mother, and because He enjoyed being with John, the son of Elizabeth and Zachary, and His other cousins, James and John, the sons of Salome and Zebedee.

When the families met again in Emmaus, Mary rushed from her relatives' house to greet Joseph.

"Where is Yeshua?" she asked, with a huge smile on her face.

"Is He not with you?"

The two parents looked at each other, and sheer panic and terror raced across their faces. For the first time in public, Joseph reached for Mary and they embraced. They both began to cry aloud. The family immediately tried to calm the stricken parents, but it was hopeless, for they were inconsolable.

Within Joseph and Mary raged different fears. Mary had lost the Son of God. She was for the first time in her life, so to speak, without God. Joseph was in fear of God for he had lost the King of the Jews. They both felt like failures and traitors to the will of God.

Cleopas and Zebedee immediately took charge. It was decided that Zebedee and the bulk of the families would continue on to Nazareth in case Jesus, after realizing He was lost, had traveled with other members of the family. Cleopas, Joseph, Mary, and James, Cleopas's oldest son, would return to Jerusalem and search for Jesus. Assuredly, Cleopas and Zebedee insisted, Jesus was with someone He knew. Being a smart young Man, He would have returned to one of the houses where they had stayed, and was waiting for their return. The logic and deductions of Cleopas and Zebedee did nothing to calm Mary and Joseph.

They returned to Jerusalem and visited the homes of several friends and associates but no one had seen Jesus. They went to businesses and places that they had visited for the holiday and did not find Him. Joseph and Mary grew more grief stricken as they desperately searched, clinging to each other like two terrified children. They tried to show strength for each other, but neither had confidence in their attempts. Jesus had been missing for three days. Finally, James, the son of Cleopas, suggested with assurance that they go to the Temple.

"We should go and pray to El Shaddai for help. In the calmness of the Temple, I am certain we can get our wits together. And perhaps Yeshua went to the Temple also."

They rushed to the Temple, entering through the *Shusuan* Gate on the Eastern Wall. To their right was Solomon's Porch. As they approached the Court of the Gentiles, they heard the sound of loud voices in heated debate. There, sitting in the midst of doctors, scribes, priest, rabbis, Pharisees, and Sadducees was young Jesus. Some of the Temple authorities were rifling through rolled scrolls and open scrolls on a nearby table. Jesus sat calmly asking questions, answering questions, and debating with great confidence and conviction. Through the confusion and shouting, Joseph heard expressions of astonishment from these learned men as to the wisdom of Jesus's answers.

A great sigh of relief escaped Joseph's being. The discovery of Jesus delivered them from the feelings of fear, abandonment and failure.

Before anyone could stop her, Mary rushed toward the gathering. With relief and yet disappointment in her voice, she asked: "Son, why hast Thou done so to us? Behold Thy father and I have sought Thee sorrowing."

Jesus turned to His mother and with a flicker of surprise on His Face said, "How is it that thou sought Me? Did ye not know that I was to be about My Father's business?"

Mary reeled back with shock at Jesus's words. She had lost her ability to speak. She understood the words Jesus had spoken, but was startled by His carefree and sudden public declaration. She glanced at Joseph. His eyes were lowered; his face was marred with confusion. When he looked up and saw Mary searching his face, he grew embarrassed and turned his eyes away. It was obvious he had been offended. In that instant Mary realized that Joseph was not fully aware of Who Jesus was.

Softly she said, "Yeshua, please excuse Thyself and come with us."

Cleopas and his son James looked on in bewilderment. Jesus's words were so unexpected and so untrue. They couldn't believe how softly Jesus had been reprimanded by His mother and how little Joseph, His father, had done or said.

They abruptly left for Nazareth. On their journey all were quiet with their own thoughts and perplexities, but none more perplexed than Joseph.

What did Yeshua mean "about His Father's business"? What did His speaking to the Temple authorities have to do with woodcutting? What manner of talk was this?

When they arrived home in Nazareth, everyone returned to their own vocation. Everything returned to normal but not normalcy. Joseph seemed distant and confused. He seldom spoke to anyone and when he did speak, it was in short quick sentences.

Mary knew he was bothered and overwhelmed. She felt a great pity for him and knew she had to do something. She prayed and sought guidance from God.

She knew her prayers would be answered because they always were. Ever since the day the Angel of the Lord came to her, whenever she prayed she received an answer. Sometimes it was not what she had asked for, but God's will was always perfect. When she thought Joseph would divorce her, she prayed; when they could not find lodging, when the shepherds came, when the Magi came, when the flight into Egypt came, she prayed; when they could not find Jesus, she prayed; and she received an answer each time. She knew that the Lord was with her and that He would always guide and assist her when she was in need.

Soon after her prayer for direction was uttered, she knew what she must do. She proceeded with a heavy heart, for she now knew that Joseph had never fully understood Who Jesus was. This was not his fault. She walked slowly and softly into the woodshop. She found Joseph standing by his work table, his strong calloused hands gripping the ends of it. He was looking off into the distance, his face twisted with perplexity. She could see the hurt etched on it, and recognized his deep sadness.

She walked to a small stool by the table and reached for his hand. Her touch jolted him from his thoughts.

"Is all well? Are you ill? Is Yeshua well?"

She smiled and let the touch of her hand on his relax him.

He glanced down at Mary's hand and the warmth from her hand settled his questions.

Mary said in a low, tender tone, "Yosef, it is time to talk."

Joseph knew she had something important to say to him and he was willing to listen.

"Yosef, you are a silent man. You speak, but never of yourself; yet your thoughts are always filled with questions. Questions you never ask or speak. Now we must speak of your questions and give you answers. Also, we must learn many things from you."

Mary searched Joseph's face and saw a man who once was filled with satisfaction and acceptance, but now looked abandoned. All the excitement and joy that she had seen on his face and which had radiated from his body was now gone. He looked lost and adrift.

She closed her eyes and asked her angel to help her speak words of clarity. "Yosef, when you came to my house many years ago to announce your willingness to marry me, you told my mother a story of a visiting angel."

He looked at her in surprise. He had not thought his mother-in-law, Anna, had repeated the story he told her, but understanding the closeness between mother and daughter, he smothered his amazement. Angels did not ordinarily appear to young men, especially with a command to marry. He almost wanted to deny the dream because he didn't want Mary to feel that the only reason he had married her was obedience to the angel.

"I believe that story," Mary continued. "And now we must speak of that dream and your angel's message."

Suddenly the dream, that had been almost forgotten, became extremely important.

"Please tell me exactly what your angel said."

Slowly he proceeded to tell her of his first dream with Malach.

"Is that all that was said to you? Did you not question this angel?"

"No, why should I? I was so happy that I did not have to disgrace you or your family, and that I had been given a mission by El Shaddai. I was given a great assignment: to help Yeshua with His mission. I would not have dared ask anything of El Shaddai's messenger."

"I did." She said. Her words hung in the air, not because they were defiant but because they nullified his choice. "I had to, because I knew that I could not break my vow."

Mary stopped, then calmly resumed: "Allow me to tell you of my angel." Slowly, with carefully chosen words, she told Joseph of Gabriel, and as she relayed the story, the past became the present. All the details of that long ago day became real again. She smelled the pleasant scent that permeated the room when Gabriel became visible. She felt the great power that filled the room and wrapped around her, making it nearly impossible for her to breathe deeply or to move her thoughts to anything else. She was not afraid; instead she was filled with reassurance. She felt the still, substantial presence of peace, and the warmth—the same warmth that she believed had existed on the day of creation.

When Gabriel spoke, she, in her innocence, became confused and wondered what sort of message this was. She realized that her confusion and astonishment were out of place at that moment, in that room; this was not a time for such things. She grasped that this was a time for great secret jubilance. Simultaneously, she understood the pause in time; all of creation waited for her to agree to the words of Gabriel. Overwhelmed by what was said, she felt the heavy, great burden of responsibility and the soft weightlessness of humility in her soul.

She accepted Gabriel's announcement, and immediately felt a soft flood of light slowly swell inside her. A bright beam penetrated her and settled deep within. In mysterious silence, the light brightened. She was sure that the light radiated from the room in which she sat. It slipped unseen to the outside the world, announcing to the unconscious that creation had begun again, that life's meaning had been intensified, and that God was forming in mortal flesh.

She described all these things to Joseph, and recognized that he was in complete awe of the experience. She grasped that he had moved and lived out of simple faith these many years. This greatly humbled her for she believed that his faith was greater than hers, assuredly nobler than hers. Her love for him, her understanding of him, grew significantly stronger, and she was thankful to God for having given him to her and for giving her the duty to tell him all.

In an instant, a sense of God—a consciousness that He was within her—made her utter a prayer: a song of thanksgiving. She continued: "…And I said to the angel 'How can this be done, because I know not man?' And the angel answered and said to me: 'Ruach Hako'desh— the Holy Spirit—shall come upon thee, and the power of El Elyon—the Most High God—shall overshadow thee. And therefore also Qadowsh—the Holy One— which shall be born of thee shall be called Ben Ha Elohim—the Son of God.'"

Mary stopped. She looked at Joseph, expecting a reaction, but none came. He stared at her with a look of numbness, then disbelief and confusion, and finally of fear. He staggered under the weight and power of her words; he gripped his work table to steady himself.

"Yosef—"

He raised his hand to silence her, his eyes glued to her face.

Mary could feel the thoughts, the questions, and the reliving of their lives together racing through his mind.

Abruptly, after a long silence, he shook his head, as if shaking himself free of any doubts. With a voice soaked in understanding, he said, "I have no reason to doubt you, Miryam. I knew Yeshua was a Messenger and expected to do great things. I believed He was to be a great rabbi, or the greatest of Prophets and the new king of our people, but the Ben Ha Elohim—Son of God!"

He fell onto a bench nearby. He again looked long and hard at Mary and asked in bewilderment, "Why us? Why me?"

"Yosef...I do not know." Her face was serious, her voice sympathetic. "I only know that El Shaddai always picks the lowest of the low to do His bidding. You—we —must have found great favor with Him. We have been given an important task to do for Him. I do not know any more than what I have told you; therefore, I do not know what our task is but I am certain Yeshua knows. I only know that we both consented out of complete trust and faith and this has pleased Him greatly. Truly the open Hand of El Shaddai is upon us."

"How am I to act? I have no great mind with which to advise Yeshua. What am I supposed to say or do? Suppose I say—do—something wrong? What happens then?"

"I do not know the answer to your questions. All I know is that we must use what El Shaddai gives us. We must trust in El Shaddai in all we do. I know that He shall not give us more than we can understand or more than we can do."

She watched Joseph's face. "I know you are still perplexed, Yosef, and your confusion must be settled between you and El Shaddai."

"But you have given Him bone, flesh and body," Joseph said simply.

"I gave Him a human body for His human existence. He is of El Shaddai. I gave Yeshua bodily needs, bodily feelings, bodily pain."

"What have I…what can I give Him?"

The question hung between them. It was so enormous and heavy that it pushed them away from each other and placed them into two different worlds, two different places. Mary gathered her strength and with great poise said in a voice of great authority, "Heritage. Human comfort and security. Respect as a creature of El Shaddai. For Heaven knows Yeshua may not receive so much from others."

Joseph looked at Mary for a long time. *How had she gotten so wise? Although she knew more of what was happening, she still had a lot of unknowns in her life. She had faith strong enough to move the immoveable.*

New thoughts flashed across his mind. They grew so heavy, so intense, that Joseph was forced to lower his head. He felt a bright light flood his mind and his being. The light was so penetrating that Joseph squinted his eyes. With great affirmation he blurted out, "And He was 'about His Father's business'!" Mary looked at her husband and felt his revelation, his humanity, and his humility. She silently thanked God, for now Joseph knew.

The room was dark, yet Joseph saw Jesus clearly. Even though he was across the room from Him, Joseph could tell that Jesus was sleeping. He looked in the direction of Mary's mat and knew she also was sleeping. Resting on his side, Joseph placed his arm under his head and tried to sleep. It did not take him long to concede that sleep would not be his. He knew he had many things to think about before sleep would become his companion. It seemed proper that he be awake to watch over his family. It was now, more than ever his duty.

After his talk with Mary, his understanding was clearer, but still he wondered about other things. He resolved that he would never have all the answers to the plan that God had laid out for him and his wife.

I have so many things I yet need to know. His eyes traveled through the dark room and settled on Jesus. *I know now who You are, but still, Yeshua, I do not know what I am to do for You. It seems that You will help me more than I will help You.*

Jesus moved, and Joseph held his breath and closed his eyes to pretend sleep. Suddenly he realized how foolish he was.

Yeshua is the Ben Ha Elohim—He knows all things and knows what game I play.

He opened his eyes and stared at Jesus, who had settled and returned to sleep.

Someday soon, You must tell me what El Shaddai looks like. You know I am very fearful of Him, for it is written that no one who sees the face of El Shaddai lives, but if You tell me what He looks like that would not be seeing Him. I cannot judge His features, because You have Your mother's face, so I must ask You to tell me what El Shaddai looks like.

Then he felt disrespectful and impudent.

"Forgive me for being bold and foolish, but I am curious," he said in a whisper, then again closed his eyes and faked sleep.

Yeshua, you must tell me what I am to do, for I have been in the shadows and ignorant of what was happening. I do not think I have been successful in doing things for the Ben Ha Elohim. Forgive my clumsy attempts in the past to make things good and perfect for You. I am an ordinary man. I cannot teach You for You know all things as El Shaddai does. What You did and said in the Temple were not of me, but of El Shaddai. What You will do in the future, will not be of me, but of El Shaddai.

How do I address You? When I pray, do I pray to You? When I ask a question about what happens to us will You give me El Shaddai's answer? Will You make it stop raining when I need a clear day to deliver my wares to my customers?

He found he was being foolish and acknowledged: *Truly Ben Ha Elohim has more important things to do than doing favors for me.*

He felt finite, imperfect and unworthy.

As You can see, Yeshua, though I know who You are, I still have questions. What do You think of me? It seems to me that I have failed You many times already. Am I too poor to provide the best? I still question why I was chosen for this plan. What did El Shaddai see in me that made me be chosen? Why do I not see what He sees? What am I to do now? Help me to see my worth.

Returning his eyes to Jesus, he stared at the Figure that he now knew was the Son of God. He turned his thoughts to the Father of his Son.

I will do all You ask of me, El Shaddai. I will try to do more and be better. Help me to understand how Your Son

*can be born human. Why would You do such a thing? I
was told He was to save His people from sin. How is that
to happen? How will He save this stiff-necked people You
call Your own, Your Chosen People?*

He broke his trend of thought with a loud sigh. He
glanced at Jesus, fearful that his sigh may have broken
Jesus's sleep, but He did not wake. He turned his head
slightly and glanced over at Mary across the room from
him. She slept.

He marveled that she was the mother to both God
and Man. This thought caused him uneasiness. He
knew that she was different: that she undoubtedly was
chosen for a greater duty than he.

*She will be seen in the eyes of the Jews as another
Ruth or Esther. In the eyes of God, she will be even
greater—perhaps she will be one of the greatest beings in
His creation.*

His heart beat rapidly as Mary's importance grew
greater in his imagination and he became lesser, and he
peacefully, gratefully accepted it.

*I shall remain her husband. Nothing more; I need
nothing more. I shall provide her security and compan-
ionship. Nothing more, nothing less. To Yeshua, I shall be
His visual father, which apparently was my only qual-
ification for being picked. My fatherhood is what was
needed and what has made me part of this family. I am
to give Yeshua a normal family existence for His human
nature. I am not like His mother who gave Him blood,
and bones, and flesh; who mothered, nourished Him in
her womb and from her breast.*

Closing his eyes tightly he felt a new and different
peace come over him; it was one he had never experienced before. He was free—empty. Suddenly, he felt

naked in this emptiness; he was in a place that made him know and understand that he was in the presence of God. He felt he was being purified and set free of all burdens and complications. He stayed in this place for a long time, and when he was beyond saturation, he, with acceptance, whispered aloud: "This is my lot, and this is what I shall do for You, El Shaddai. I beg You to accept the love I have for Your Son as my love for You."

At peace with himself, Joseph closed his mind, knowing that sleep would soon be his mate. Then he heard from the other side of the room a small voice say: "Lailah tov, Av. Toda Lecha—Good night, father, thank you."

In the darkness, Joseph's eyes grew wet with tears of happiness.

The next day, Joseph woke with a great feeling of triumph. For the first time in years, he felt he knew who he was and why he was. The fears he had had the night before of being the caretaker of Jesus, the Son of God, had been erased with the night's sleep. He was happy for he knew his place in Jesus's life.

He was aware he was alone in the house. Mary and Jesus had gone to the small Nazarene fruit market to get provisions. So he set about to begin his day, but before beginning his work day, he gave thanks to God for all His benefits. As he entered prayer, he raised his hands to Heaven, lifted his eyes to the open blue sky, and became fixed on one thought. All his life as a servant of God, he had looked up to the heavens to his God. God had always been above him, and now God had willed that His Son live on earth. He, Who had rested in Joseph's arms, had clung to Joseph's legs, had been fed by Joseph's hand, and now walked, talked, sat and lived in Joseph's home, was the Son of God. Now he, Joseph, the son of Adam, the son of David and Jacob, the son of humanity could look down at his Child, his God. This was not to be! Joseph vowed from that day on he would bend or stoop, so that Jesus, the Son of God, would not have to look up to him.

As time passed, this respect was noticed by Jesus and Mary. Each time Joseph did this small act of homage, Jesus would smile. Joseph understood that his "Son" knew why he did what he did.

As the years passed, there were times that Joseph wanted to ask Jesus questions. When a neighbor's daughter died, he wanted to ask Him why God had demanded the life of so young and beautiful a daughter. When the Romans raised taxes, he wanted to ask Him why the Jews had to suffer so much. When crops failed, when it did not rain, when people became ill, he wanted to ask why, but he never did.

Many times he was tempted to ask Jesus what His Father looked like; He wanted to ask Him how King David had looked, or how Moses had looked. He wanted to know if God had helped Noah get two of a kind into the ark. What did the Angel of Death look like on the first Passover? What was Eden like? How did it feel to know all things? But he never asked and therefore never learned the answers.

While Jesus was young, Mary and Joseph guided Him, instructed Him and nurtured Him. They watched Jesus become the binder in their families. He always mended problems between the relatives. He was always helping His neighbors, and often repaired things for them without them asking and without being paid. They expected this of Jesus for they knew He was all-good, and the Son of Love, mercy and care. Joseph never objected. When Jesus saw the poor, the sick or the lame, He did whatever He could to give them physical comfort. Joseph and Mary understood why He did this and often followed Him, knowing that they also were doing the will of God. When Sabbath arrived, He was always first to be ready for synagogue, and always the last to leave the house of prayer. When they arrived home for Sabbath dinner, His face glowed for hours.

Many years later, on *Chanukah*—the Feast of Lights, they made a trip to Jerusalem with their extended family. They enjoyed the holiday as usual with family and laughter and holiness. On the last day of their visit, the family witnessed the crucifixion of an insurrectionist. It distressed everyone, and when they voiced their anger and condemnation of Rome, Jesus tried to calm them with words of forgiveness and love. Later in the day, Joseph found Jesus tracing the figure of a cross on the sand in front of the house where they were staying. He wondered if Jesus was more disturbed by what had happened than he suspected.

"Did what You saw today bother You greatly, Yeshua?"

"No, not really."

"Then why do You occupy Yourself with drawing those images in the sand?"

"Because I must learn the meaning of all things and for this reason I must know the meaning of the cross."

Once again, Jesus had spoken in a way Joseph did not understand, but he never questioned Him or sought an explanation from Him. Joseph knew that if he was meant to know, then it would be made known. On that same day, Jesus and Joseph found themselves together walking through the narrow streets of the city.

Suddenly Jesus said, "In this city, years from now, I shall suffer much."

"Why do You say that, Yeshua? This is a Holy City."

"It is. And it will always be a Holy City and I shall make it holier. I shall bring it great glory and it shall be remembered by many people far and near, but it also shall have a scar upon it that will linger long."

"At times I do not understand what You say or why You say the things you say."

"All that I say shall come to pass, Av—father."

For the first time in their relationship, the word "father" held a chill. Joseph felt that time was closing in on him and that he was not going to be a part of what Jesus was to do. He knew that Jesus would never be disrespectful, but He had just made a prophecy. Joseph knew that he would someday not only know the meaning of these words, but that he would be forced to live them. Jesus turned to Joseph and looked sadly at him. Joseph wanted to seek clarification of Jesus's words. He also wanted to shout a protest, to demand or beg that the words he had heard would never be, but the objections slipped away.

It is the will of El Shaddai, he thought, and slowly the tide of his husbandhood and fatherhood receded, and he became a servant of his God.

Jesus broke eye contact and turning to his right, He pointed to a young boy with red hair, wearing an expensive robe.

"You see that young boy, Av Yosef?"

Joseph looked. The boy was Jesus's age, but far more fashionably dressed, in a long white robe trimmed with purple, which told that the boy was of royal lineage.

"Someday that boy shall be one of My chosen ones. He shall be an Apostle of the Lord and he shall travel far for Me. In his old age he shall even die for me."

"Yeshua, who is that young man and how do you know these things?"

Jesus did not answer him but continued walking. Finally, He paused and said, "That young man over there will come to help Me in My loneliest hour. And this young man walking by us will be remembered in history as the one on whom I performed my last kindness." Joseph looked at Jesus and grew sad. He again felt distanced from the purpose of Jesus's earthly mission. He had not had this feeling in many years but now it was fresh, and its newness frightened him and hurt him deeply. He felt alone. Curiously, his thoughts traveled, and he imagined that this was the way Moses felt when he was told he would not see the Promised Land.

But Moses had not trusted El Shaddai; he had disobeyed Him. I have not done either.

He wondered if all his years of questioning, of being unsure, of feeling inadequate had finally demanded El Shaddai's attention.

Joseph was about to ask Jesus to explain all that was passing between them when Jesus again spoke, "Be not frightened, Av Yosef, and do not feel alone, for soon you will have many around you whom you know, and they will be of great comfort to you."

The moment was broken when the air filled with the sounds of marching Roman soldiers and galloping legionnaire horses. Everyone scurried away from the

road and the on-coming charge. Some pressed themselves against the walls of nearby buildings and held
their breaths. After the Romans had passed, Joseph
looked for Jesus but could not find Him in the crowd.
He craned his neck and stood on his toes searching for
Him, but He was not to be found. Joseph knew that
Jesus was old enough to find His way back to their relative's house, but this did not stop him from worrying.
Again, he glanced quickly around the area, and when
he could not find Jesus, he rushed back to their lodgings. As he neared the house, he saw Jesus standing on
a hill behind it between two tall trees. Joseph strode
toward Him, but it seemed that he could not draw near
to Jesus or reach Him. Then Jesus raised His Arms and
His Body cast a long shadow from the hill to where
Joseph stood. Joseph looked down at the shadow and
his heart leapt in fear, for before him, on the ground,
the shadow of Jesus formed a cross. Joseph understood
all that Jesus had said during their walk. He closed his
eyes and felt a sharp pain pierce his body. The pain
was so severe that he almost lost his footing. When
he opened his eyes, Jesus was standing before him. He
immediately stooped so as not to be above Jesus.

"Fear not, Av Yosef, for you will be spared the
images I speak of, and that shall be your blessing. That
which is to happen was never for you to know, for they
were meant for Me and My mother to experience and
know."

These words caused Joseph to sway. He knew the
meaning of these words. He shook his head violently
in denial but he could not speak. He wanted to know
when he would be called by God. He wanted to know
why he again was not part of the plan. Jesus rested His

hand on Joseph's head. Instead of begging for Mary to be spared, instead of pleading to be allowed to witness all that was to happen, instead of imploring for more time, Joseph gently slipped into a state of complete peace and relinquished his will to that of God.

Several weeks later Joseph became ill and bed-ridden. Jesus and Mary attended him day and night. Throughout his last ordeal, Joseph remained complacent and in constant prayer. His life and sufferings became a prayer. His prayers were not for himself but for Mary, who he believed would need strength in the future. What he knew of the future hurt him and now it was his turn to remain silent and let God's will be done.

For many days Joseph suffered great pain. He knew his pains were nothing in comparison to the agony that Jesus and Mary were to endure. He often glanced at Jesus, hoping to see some sign of reassurance that all would not be as severe as he imagined. He prayed to Jesus to bestow strength and a gentle hand to Mary in her future sufferings. He begged that she have peace of mind and calm of heart in the years after his departure. Finally, as he neared his time, he turned to Jesus and mentally begged for strength to accept his own death. He was unsure of the challenge he was to face. He knew that Jesus could save him, but he also knew that this was not the time for Jesus to declare Himself—that would come later when God allowed it. He looked back and determined that life lived without purpose was more of a chore than a delight. He understood that throughout his life, he had weighed himself down with the things of life: habits, thoughts, pride, selfishness or disrespect. He slowly began to rid himself of all that was once his and began to feel a degree of freedom. A few days later Joseph awoke and felt a great serenity. In this calm, he knew that this was his day: the day of the end. He noted in his thoughts that it was the month of *Asar*—March—and he thought of all the months of March that he had lived plainly doing what was his to do, yet never realizing that this month was marked for his death. He then remembered all the days that he had lived ignorant of Who Jesus was, and he looked at his Son with eyes that begged forgiveness.

I was only human with little knowledge and not much of anything to give You. Have I done what was pleasing to You? Will You still remember me as Your father?

Mary asked him if he wanted some water and he nodded his head. She quickly left, leaving Joseph and Jesus alone.

Jesus tenderly placed his hand on Joseph's chest and said, "It is time, Av Yosef. Go in peace, for you have been a just and faithful servant of My Abba in Heaven. I shall come for you later and will give you great praise."

Jesus stood upright, extended His arms over Joseph, and began to chant:

"Av harachameem shochein m'romeem, b'rachamav ha-atzumeem hu yeefkod b'rachamim.

The Father of mercy who dwells on high in His great

mercy will remember with compassion the pious,

upright and blameless."

Mary returned to the room with a small cup of water. She went to Joseph and lifted his head to make it easier for him to drink. Jesus assisted her, and with both their arms about him, Joseph drank his cup and closed his eyes. Two tears slowly inched their way down his cheeks. They were not tears of regret or of surrender; these last tears were for Jesus and Mary: they were tears of compassion and thanksgiving.

Joseph was walking casually, freely down a wide-open endless passage.

It was a road without form, and for a moment, Joseph believed it was not a road at all. It was a special path made just for him, and he felt compelled to walk this road. There was no sound of life around him, only softness, tender quiet and endless openness. As he continued, he strangely began to feel a softness, quietness and openness press against him, and soon he was engulfed and clothed by this feeling. This surprised him for he hadn't known that he could feel these abstract things.

For an instant, he felt completely alone. This aloneness was so great that it oppressed him and left him in complete desolation, but as quickly as the feeling came over him, it dissipated. He looked at the long road before him and all he saw was thick clouds. He glanced down at his feet, and they were covered by a heavy mist. He wondered if they were there and if they truly were moving.

"Shalom, Yosef."

"Shalom," Joseph automatically replied, and looked to his side to see his angel Malach. Joseph smiled for the angel was now an old friend, a restful companion and fellow traveler.

"We walk together on another road," Malach said.

"But this is an unusual road. I have never walked on a road such as this."

"What is so unusual?"

"I do not grow tired on it. I walk with no help, no staff. It is comfortable, and yet mysterious. I know it and am happy to be on it."

"It is just a road, yet unlike other roads, this one is taken by all. No one escapes this road or avoids this walk."

They walked on in silence, and as they walked the silence grew dense.

"Many people await you, Yosef."

"Strange, but I know what you say is true. I feel their friendship and love all around me."

"Here all is love and friendship; there is nothing else. No faith is needed. No hope is needed, just love and all things that make love live."

Suddenly the fog grew thicker. It embraced him, making it impossible for him to walk further. Joseph could not breathe. He felt himself panic. He needed air. He needed to breathe. Then he felt a sharp pain in his chest.

Shrouded with nothing but fog, nothing but whiteness, he experienced completeness and unlimited happiness.

Surprisingly, Joseph lost the need to breathe. He was freed from air and all other needs.

He heard Malach say, "Yosef bar Yakov of Nazareth. Your road finally ends. Hakkadosh Barukh Hu—The Holy One—awaits you for He has much to say to you and much for which to thank you."

It was a place that had no limits and no doubts. It was a place full of nothing and yet everything. It was a place filled with songs and humming, a place of rest and light and softness. All was so gentle that it called you to sleep, though no one needed to sleep. It left Joseph in the state of no need, for all that was needed was there, present, accompanying him everywhere he walked. In this place he knew everything; he knew everyone. He knew questions and understood answers. He walked and never spoke a word, yet gave greetings and heard greetings. In this place, his past life was spoken of as one yesterday, and yesterdays were today, and today was forever, and the future was now. It was a place of completed journeys and ended pilgrimages.

In this place he saw men and women of known greatness, of known service, walking about with no idea of how great they had been. He saw people—common people—who did nothing and gave nothing yet were now great.

He was reunited with family, relatives, and ancestors. Many he had never seen before, but he knew them and they knew him. He was reacquainted with friends, neighbors, associates. He saw people who had passed him and pressed against him in his yesterdays. He saw forgotten, unknown people, and momentary people. He saw people who had caused a quick breeze to stir the air around him in life and who meant nothing to him when they passed, but now were important to him.

Suddenly one yesterday, many years later in earthly time, this place changed. Everything became unsettled. A reechoing rumble was heard. A loud roll rushed over the place. Everyone stopped, and knew something had happened, and that what had happened was serious. It came from the end of the road on the other side. Turmoil and pain and trouble existed there; tears and moans originated there. It was where time was everything. Often they had heard the cries, the calls and the supplications, but now, this time, it was very close to them and they sensed it was all for them.

Joseph felt dampness around him, and an unfamiliar chill. He knew without seeing or hearing that tears were being shed. He felt and understood a great sadness around them. In the silence, he knew that each of them felt desolation. Again, it came from the other side. The only thing they could do was go to the main room where they often went to give praise and declare petitions.

They milled around the main room waiting, sensing a great moment—a moment so great that time in the other place was stilled and time in their place was holding its breath.

They waited and waited and waited.

A strong wind rushed by them; a thunderous rolling sound passed over them. A light brighter than any light ever known to have shone before came over them. They knew this light was equal to the light of the first days of creation. Embraced in this light, they heard a long loud aspiration, an exhale of relief and new life.

Joseph looked up from his place in the back of the room knowing, as the others did, what all this was about.

Jesus was before them. He appeared from the light and the light stayed with Him as He walked into the room. Immediately, intense softness, peace and blamelessness filled and crowded the room. As He passed those in the room, they began to inhale afresh, and their face flushed with great newness.

He continued his walk. He passed Moses, Joshua, Judith, Isaiah, Esther, Jeremiah, Micah, Ruth, and Sirach. His scent permeated the senses of Jacob and Eva, Anna and Joachim, Zachary and Elizabeth and their son John. He walked by many other greats and not so greats. They all stepped aside as He continued to the back of the room and finally came to a stop before Joseph. Joseph raised his eyes and looked at his Glorified God. He bowed to Him and asked, "How is Your mother?"

Mary sat in a small chair. She was not feeling well. She knew she was being prepared for her step over the threshold and her new life with God. But that would come later, for now she had to find the strength to answer the needy questions of Luke, the physician. He came to her to fill in the many blank spaces in his account of Jesus's early life. As she told him of her angel's visit, her trip to see her cousin Elizabeth, the shepherds' arrival, Simeon's prophecy, the trip into Egypt, the losing of Jesus and then the finding, she relived all the excitements, fears, joys and obediences of those times. She enjoyed watching the glow of excitement on Luke's face as she told him of those early hidden days. Luke was like a child who had just discovered the use of his hands and feet.

Luke clutched his jaws tightly to keep from crying out with joy. He marveled as he watched Mary's face grow young as she recalled the past times. He was exalted by her faith and by her humility and knew that he would never totally capture these virtues in his writings of Jesus. They were only for Mary; they belonged only to her.

Perhaps this is something I am not meant to do. Perhaps the future will discover this for themselves, as I and others have had to discover, Luke thought.

He asked another question and again she continued the story, void of self-praise.

It is all about Jesus and rightly so, Luke thought again.

When he had all the information that he wanted, he found he did not want to leave her, so he began asking about her health and other less important things. He suggested to Joanna of Chiusa to boil some herbs to give her more comfort. Finally he began to take his leave, but he wanted to ask one more question.

She had told him so much about Jesus, and without a word, had told him much about herself.

"Leidi Miryam—Lady Mary, tell me, what was Yosef bar Yakov like?"

A new and different glow came to Mary's face. After a few moments, a small, warm smile, spread across her face and she grew younger still. She softly wet her lips.

Luke saw tears sit on the brim of her eyelids but he knew they were tears of pride and great love.

"Yosef." She spoke with a softness that held great esteem and strength. Luke knew that the name stood alone, and even before Lady Mary continued, he knew he was about to hear of greatness.

Mary looked to the nearby window. Her sight and mind were endless and ageless. Finally, in a tender voice, she said, "Yosef was a just man. A righteous man. A great servant." Then with understanding and respect on her face, she took a deep breath, brought her body upright, and continued, "Yosef was a loving father."

JMJ

T

 **About Leonine Publishers**

Leonine Publishers LLC makes fine Catholic literature available to Catholics throughout the English-speaking world. Leonine Publishers offers an innovative "hybrid" approach to book publication that helps authors as well as readers. Please visit our web site at www.leoninepublishers.com to learn more about us. Browse our online bookstore to find more solid Catholic titles to uplift, challenge, and inspire.

Our patron and namesake is Pope Leo XIII, a prudent, yet uncompromising pope during the stormy years at the close of the 19th century. Please join us as we ask his intercession for our family of readers and authors.

Do you have a book inside you? Visit our web site today. Leonine Publishers accepts manuscripts from Catholic authors like you. If your book is selected for publication, you will have an active part in the production process. This book is an example of our growing selection of literature for the busy Catholic reader of the 21st century.

www.leoninepublishers.com